Denis Muoria is an author with deep appreciation for fictional literary work, cinema, crafted cocktails, and curious minds that constantly debate the fictional 'what-if' factors.

Aiding in endeavour to complete the work, Denis says, was a favourite concoction of coffee and absinthe; Negronis, accompanied by a serious case of insomnia that saw him awake at odd hours of the night on his writer's desk, working on his manuscript while listening to Chopin's Nocturnes on repeat. The author hopes you enjoy the read and recommend it to a friend.

Denis Muoria

GENEVIEVE – BOOK I

AUSTIN MACAULEY PUBLISHERS™
LONDON · CAMBRIDGE · NEW YORK · SHARJAH

Copyright © Denis Muoria 2022

The right of Denis Muoria to be identified as author of this work has been asserted by the author in accordance with section 77 and 78 of the Copyright, Designs and Patents Act 1988.

All rights reserved. No part of this publication may be reproduced, stored in a retrieval system, or transmitted in any form or by any means, electronic, mechanical, photocopying, recording, or otherwise, without the prior permission of the publishers.

Any person who commits any unauthorised act in relation to this publication may be liable to criminal prosecution and civil claims for damages.

This is a work of fiction. Names, characters, places and incidents are either a product of the author's imagination or are used fictitiously. Any resemblance to actual persons, living or dead, or to actual events or locales is purely coincidental.

A CIP catalogue record for this title is available from the British Library.

ISBN 9781398482869 (Paperback)
ISBN 9781398482876 (ePub e-book)

www.austinmacauley.com

First Published 2022
Austin Macauley Publishers Ltd®
1 Canada Square
Canary Wharf
London
E14 5AA

Chapter I
New Genesis

She stood in front of her dressing mirror half nude as she powdered her nose, preparing herself for yet another day, staring at her reflection, displeased at what she saw as she had been over the years. Unlike other women, she hoped to find flaws, embracing any she might have picked up on and disappointed in the lack of 'blemishes, wrinkles, or a scar.' She subconsciously whispered her thoughts beneath her breath as she looked desperately for anatomical changes on her body to bear testament to all her years on Earth, the proverbial lean to her Tower of Pisa, for just like the leaning tower, she had stood the test of time, her hair as dark as an eclipse night, a figure that would make an atheist believe in God, and skin as smooth as the twenty-five-year-old scotch she consumed the night before on her latest escapade.

"Come back to bed," a deep masculine voice interrupted her train of thoughts which at the time mostly consisted of self-loathing. She turned back to get a good look at her lover from the previous night. She had so many over the past weeks and did not want to embarrass both herself and her lover by addressing him by the wrong name.

"I enjoyed myself, though I think it's time for you to go." She rejected his indirect invitation to make love as politely and as directly as she could.

Shortly after getting dressed, her guest walked up to her and kissed her on the cheek. "Goodbye, Genevieve," he whispered and she watched as he walked away, knowing that she would never see him again. She sighed in relief when the elevator doors shut behind him.

She got ready to leave for the office, pushed the button on the elevator to her penthouse, and got in, grabbing a copy of the daily newspaper in the lobby as she made it to the exit. Her chauffeur was waiting for her at the front of her building as always. He held the door for her. "Good morning, Miss Henrietta," he said with a smile on his face. She smiled back and got in the car. They drove off.

It was a new day and Genevieve Henrietta was on the brink of acquiring a business contract from the city which would see her soar up to the status quo of one the most successful women in the world. It truly was an exciting period of time for her, though she was anything but that. Her previous failed encounters with ultimate success had left her jaded and cold to the thought to a point where she was quoted saying, "I shall be disappointed if I fail but not surprised," a quote that was heavily associated with her celebrity as it trended and became subject to many witty responses.

She did not require validation. On the contrary, anonymity was more of her heart's desire, of which we seldom get. Her instincts to claw her way up to the top of the 'success pyramid' were undeniable, almost primal and natural. That set her on the opposite path of the anonymity and privacy she so desired, as her accomplishments and great feats gathered the attention of the world. Those who knew of her and her contributions to architecture in the architectural and development circles, referred to her as an apex predator, for she was intimidating, and whatever she set out to accomplish, she would, laying waste to competitors and emerging successful every time.

Those who were acquainted with her on a personal level defined Genevieve as jaded, self-absorbed, irritable, and quick to lash out, all horrible traits which would hinder anyone's success. Yet, she somehow ended up coming out on top, climbing ranks and gaining favour with very little effort from her side and a lot of assistance from men of status and power in her field, who would somehow get swayed to do whatever she pleased. Rumour had it that she had a way with men, a supernatural sway over the opposite sex that usually ended up with her at task completion and her victims, for lack of a better word, in ruination.

Her car pulled up in front of her sixty-story building that won the previous year's World's Architectural Marvels Award, an event organised by specialists in the field for recognising ingenious designs. She designed the building herself and could have just as easily put her name on it in huge blocks but that would have gone against her core beliefs and ambitions of anonymity. Instead, she branded it with the initials of her company FF, which in full stood for the FIRST FRUIT COOPERATION.

Within five years, her company had seen extensive growth with her at the helm steering the 'ship' to success with every endeavour and project they took. In the course of five years, she did what many would consider impossible, building a conglomerate that was highly recognised worldwide, all at the tender age of thirty-two; at least that was what she told the tabloids when publicly asked about her age. It was almost as if she had done this before or she had a strong sense of foresight. Her moves were well calculated and she never took a loss in her whole career. It was truly a force to be reckoned with. A gentleman dressed in a valet uniform reached for her car door and opened it for her. He caught a glimpse of her infinity-symbol tattoo on her right leg as she stepped out of the vehicle. "Good morning, Miss Henrietta," he said. She smiled and walked past him.

She walked towards the building. The doorman opened the left door for her. "Good morning, Miss Henrietta." She smiled back and walked through the massive door into the FF Tower reception. There was a water feature in the middle of the lobby and at the centre of it was a huge sculpture of a tree with what appeared to be an unidentified fruit hanging from its leaves and a serpent curled up on one of its brunches. It was of her own design and was sculpted by one of the most famous sculptors in the city. Every morning while heading to her office, she would take a moment to look at it and the employees in the lobby would remain in utter silence till she was done soaking up on the view of the sculpture, as it was a daily routine.

She stared at it as if it reminded her of simpler times. Her cell phone rang, snapping her out of her daydream. She took her mobile device out her pocket and glanced at the screen. A popup notification read, *"Reminder: board meeting with the mayor at 9 a.m."* She put back her phone in her left pocket and made her way to the executive elevator, unfazed by what many would perceive as an important message. Everyone she bumped into the hallways would avoid direct eye-contact and crossing her path as you would avoid an apex predator. The elevator doors shut and the mechanical contraption slung-shot her straight up to the sixtieth floor in less than thirty seconds. The building truly was state-of-the-art.

The doors opened and her personal assistant was waiting for her with a cup of takeaway herbal tea in hand from Genevieve's favourite cafe, as was her daily morning routine. "Good morning, Miss Henrietta," she said without expecting a response as she handed her the white paper cup with brown accents.

"Good morning, Jessica," she replied. Jessica's face lit up like fireworks on New Year's Eve. It was completely out of character for Genevieve to respond to salutations in the morning. This gave her the impression that she was fond of her or at least appreciated her services, an accurate observation.

"You have quite a busy schedule ahead. The city mayor and members of the board have been waiting in the boardroom for fifteen minutes. I had a coffee and pastries station set up. They are currently gouging themselves in donuts and washing them down with a good 'cuppa' as they wait," Jessica briefed Genevieve in the corridors as they walked towards the boardroom. Genevieve was impressed by her problem-solving skills and her remark on the city's elite gouging themselves in donuts made her smile for a micro-second. Jessica held the boardroom door open for Genevieve. She walked in and the room went silent.

"Thank you all for coming today." An opening remark portraying what was clearly fake gratitude; she was unapologetic for her tardiness but everyone in that room knew if there was anyone who could arrange a meeting of the city's elite and show up fifteen minutes late, it was Genevieve Henrietta. "The reason I arranged this meeting today is to discuss the city's current outdated infrastructure as well as to announce my intentions to intervene in the designs and development of this incredible city by sharing my designs of the state-of-the-art FF tower and implementing those designs in every building that is built from now on henceforth, as well as tearing down the old ones to replace them with sturdier and slicker skyscrapers. We will turn this city into a one-of-a-kind future-forward marvel and testament to human ingenuity, bringing it to a new beginning, a new genesis."

The room was flooded by applause approving of her idea, some yelling, "Bravo!" While they clapped all at first glance, seeming to be on board with her ingenious idea, all but one, the city mayor, did not clap and applaud as the others did. Instead, he gave Genevieve a look of concern. His facial expression gave Genevieve the impression that he would not be on board with her plans for the future. He looked at her as if he was the only one who knew that her ambitions were not feasible, let alone practical. She slowly made her way towards him, shaking hands and making eye-contact with members of the board that were standing between her and the mayor. He saw her walking towards him, so he made his way towards a nearby window with a view of the city, subtly creating distance between himself and the group for a private conversation as Genevieve approached.

"Anything the matter, Patrick?" She undoubtedly was on a first-name basis with the mayor.

"Nice speech, Genevieve. Just how are you planning to accomplish this great feat? I most certainly will not back this lunacy financially or in any other way," he said with a smug face, almost as if he enjoyed turning down her insinuated proposal. 'Who does she think she is? Making such an audacious assumption that I would support such a motion. Tearing down all the city buildings gradually or simultaneously to build new ones would cost a fortune in taxpayers' money!' he thought to himself.

"Patrick, you wound me," she said flirtatiously and with a smile on her face, her simple response making him forget his frustrations and concern in the matter. He looked at her eyes. Her feminine eyelashes batted. His glance trickled down to her curvy lips and even lower to her chest. Her cleavage was showing, as she had three buttons from the top open every time she wore a blouse. Her perfectly sized and even breasts made him forget his train of thoughts. "Meet me in my corner office and I shall explain everything," she said seductively and slowly made her way towards her private office as the rest of her guests mingled over coffee and donuts. He looked at her as she walked away, her curvy hips swinging left and right, her thick thighs stretching out the slits on her black miniskirt. She was truly a vision. The mayor was a married man but, in that instant, he would have burnt down his house if Genevieve had asked.

He gave her some time to arrive and settle in the private office and soon followed. He walked with purpose. He walked with conviction. He walked to get a bite of the juicy, flavourful forbidden fruit. He walked through the translucent office door and locked it behind him. The last thing he needed was someone walking in on what was about to happen. He walked towards his own ruin.

Chapter II

"Ante omnem infirmitatem."
"All men are weak before me."

Patrick walked in and sat on the chair on the client end of her desk. It was moderately lowered compared to Genevieve's office chair as a power move, and all those who sat on it would have to look up to her to address her.

This, however, was not a professional visit. She had kicked off her pumps heels and had her legs on the table, her iconic infinity symbol tattoo on her right foot clearly visible, her long legs stretched out till the edge of the desk, and her narrow feet suspended in the air. Patrick could feel his blood rushing through his member, attempting to rip through his pants from desire of this insatiable goddess among men.

"You owe me an explanation," he said, hoping that she didn't have one and would try to win his favour by bending over and letting him thrust her womanhood to climax. She gave him a patronising look as if judging him for his weakness, the same look a peddler would give to his frequent and heavily addicted customer upon purchase of a dose that might end his life. She knew exactly what he wanted. She planted the seed of lust in his mind, a seed that had now grown into an oak full of lusty fruit ripe for the plucking.

"Your explanation is at the edge of my lips. You shall have to come closer to hear it," she said as she spread her legs one on each edge of the relatively long table. She was incredibly flexible. Patrick gulped in surprise. He had never met a woman so blunt and graceful in his entire life. Any consequences as outcome of this encounter would have been worth it. He was captivated and at her mercy.

He pushed his chair back and got to his knees. As soon as he got to the ground, he could see Genevieve's womanhood from under the desk. He crawled towards her and put his hands under her buttocks in a position of a thirsty man fetching drinking water from a fountain. He kissed her inner thigh and gradually worked his way up. She smelled like pinewood. She gasped for air as Patrick's lips found their way to the upper front part of her womanhood. He realised the more he focused on the particular area, the more positive reaction he got from her. He kept going, toiling his tongue clockwise and anti-clockwise, diagonally and horizontally, fast and slow, and vice versa, till she let out a tiny squeal of pleasure and her thighs quivered. He knew that he had her ready for penetration. He hurriedly unzipped his pants before he missed the moment and had to start all over again. He put his member in her and it slipped right in. He started slow but she grabbed him by the waist, nudging him to pick up the pace. She was almost at her orgasmic destination. She noticed he had started to slow down, so she made an exotic and dominant manoeuvre that resulted in her on top, grinding her pelvic area vigorously while bouncing up and down, and just when she noticed the mayor was about to finish his journey, she arched on him and remained on top of him, motionless. She could feel him about to unload. She looked in his eyes as he let out a grunt of pleasure. His heart started beating rapidly as they made eye-contact. "Your eyes! There is something wrong with your eyes!" The white in her eyes had turned to a horrible yellow with pitch-black vertical pupils like those of a venomous serpent!

"Ante omnem infirmitatem," she said before he could shrug and push her away from his lap.

Patrick didn't speak a word of Latin but he responded to what she chanted in a state of hypnosis, *"Ante omnes infirmi."*

"All men are weak before you." She smiled, certain that he was now under her spell and she had attained full control of his mind. She got off her mount position as he lay motionless on the retractable office chair which would have easily passed for an adulterer's bed based on what had just occurred.

She adjusted her skirt, put her shoes back on, and walked a few paces away from the mayor to gather her words. He was dazed and in a state of hypnosis. Her eyes were back to normal by the time she started walking towards him, as he sat on the office chair they made love in motionlessly.

"Patrick, on this desk is a very important document to me. I need you to sign it." She continued, "It states that you, the mayor, have given me rein and authority over infrastructure and development within city limits, to design and to build as I see fit, to relocate occupied units to tear down any building I please and bring the city to a new genesis." He grabbed his pen from his left coat pocket and reached for the document, doing her bidding like the mindless drone her sway had turned him into.

She had used her enchantment on many powerful and unsuspecting men over time and clearly did not require proof of concept on its success rate. Yet, as soon as he put down his signature, she grabbed the document hastily as if he would suddenly slip out of his euphoric trance and discover what had just happened. The stakes were too high and she left no merging for error on her most ambitious of ambitions to reform and rebuild the city to her own liking. She walked towards a painting similar to the sculpture of a tree in the lobby, a fruit and a serpent curled up on one of its brunches across the room. Grabbing it by its side frame and dismounting it from the wall exposing a safe, she put in the seven-digit code and placed the piece of paper under lock and key for safekeeping. She mounted the painting to again conceal the safe and walked towards the mayor leaning onto his seat, priming him for a whisper.

"*Tu dismissed* You are dismissed." He suddenly snapped out of his trance to find Genevieve standing in front of him, her right foot stepping on the chair he was sitting on, her iconic infinity-symbol tattoo clearly visible, and her pump shoe dangerously close to his exposed member from his unzipped pants that lay flaccid and was drained of all enthusiasm. "You can put that away now." She gave him a facade of utter satisfaction, giving the impression that he was the best lover she had ever encountered and he looked back at her and smiled like a conquering king in his vault of spoils while putting away that flaccid anatomical tool of his damnation. He adjusted his parasols and bade Genevieve farewell with a wet lustful kiss as if attempting a soul transfusion and then walked out to face the rest of his tight schedule as the mayor of the city and the pawn she knew he was.

Every time she chanted those damming words, she felt exasperated as if she lost a piece of herself and on the same token gaining favour from her unsuspecting mate to serve her objective. Waves of mixed emotions crushed on her intellectual shore as she looked down upon the city from her sixtieth-floor window, contemplating on the lengths she had to go to get to where she was and envisioned her architectural plans for the city as she soaked in endorphins from her latest sexual encounter with the mayor. It was just after midday and it was panning out to be the most industrious of many industrious days in decades. She had managed to get the equivalent if not more of the key to the city before lunch, at the rate of progression that would leave one wondering what she would have accomplish by dinner.

Her guests and members of the board were still gathered in the boardroom. She would take a moment to herself and join them to celebrate the new beginning of the company. She picked up the phone that was on the table and called her assistant. "Jessica, send bottles of champagne to the boardroom. Let John know I will be with them shortly." John handled matters of public relations for the company and was a member of the board but unofficially Genevieve's mouthpiece. He would inform the masses that Genevieve would make up on her absence with great news.

She left the privacy of her corner office and made her way to the boardroom. The previous coffee station was now a champagne stand with bottles of sparkling fermented grapes of the highest vintage. "We have had quite the morning, haven't we, boys?" she said with a smirk on her face as the crowd laughed at her very gender specific opening remark in a room with a well-balanced woman-to-man ratio. If only they knew how busy she had truly been! She revelled in the fact that everyone in the room was oblivious to her transgressions of the past hour.

"We have it, the green light to meld and shape this city to first fruit company architectural standards. The legal document naming us as beneficiaries to this huge task ahead is in my possession signed by the mayor himself." The room drowned in applause. There were many doubters and naysayers among them. Yet, they all seemed to be glad that she wasn't just blowing smoke and giving out empty rhetoric. "We will have to get a lot of work done in a relatively short period of time but this will be our best work yet and on a large scale, this will be my 'magnum opus' and you will all get to join me in the tough yet very rewarding journey." Applause seemed to be a recurring thing whenever she addressed a group of people. She knew her audience and could single each one of them out while addressing them all as a collective. Her charisma knew no bounds. "Today, we shall all take the day off to celebrate and to rest, for life will never be the same for us from today hence forth. We have our work cut out for us and I'm confident we will emerge victorious at task completion. Thank you and enjoy the champagne before getting on with the rest of your day." She dismissed the board members and thus the gathering. They walked into her building curious and concerned that she had summoned them and walked out satisfied and fulfilled by the news she gave them. If she did not have a strong intuition and sense of foresight, she would have jinxed her seamless victories by daring to celebrate them too soon, but she knew better. Nothing brings bad luck like celebrating prematurely. Yet, she felt the need to treat herself to dinner and a few drinks at her local bar. It was just about sunset and aperitive hour at 'moon crystal,' her favourite bar and restaurant. She made her way there, as she wasn't going to pass on well-crafted cocktails and the possibility of a drunken sexual encounter with a stranger.

Chapter III
'Una Vita Per Una Vita'
'A Life for a Life'

He sat at the bar counter drinking straight shots of bourbon like it was healthy for him. He did not mind that he had the collar on, nor the fact that people in the bar were looking at him with expressions of both disgust and curiosity along with some whispers that were not so inaudible. "Wonder why a priest is getting drunk at the bar, crisis of faith perhaps?" He overheard a conversation between a couple a few tables away from the barstool counter on which he was perched like a bird of prey on a branch of its favourite scouting tree, his nonchalant nature giving out the impression that public image did not faze him.

His was a tale of controversy from his rough upbringing in the city's orphanage to his adult decisions of joining the military which was the first domino to drop in a butterfly effect that eventually left him subject to a bad joke of a priest who walked into a bar and ordered bourbon. Only in this context, the priest kept ordering for bourbon like he was stuck in a terrible loop as the punch line.

In the military, he earned the Purple Heart which is the highest distinguished medal that can be given to a soldier for acts of valour and exemplary skill. His military records redacted and classified to unauthorised personnel and the few who laid eyes on it knew his talent and real calling in life was bringing death to the doorsteps of the nation's enemies.

He held the record for most kills in the military. This in general was the primary cause of his choice to turn to priesthood, partially to ease his conscience for all the lives he had taken and in the same tune providing spiritual guidance to his flock with hope of redemption at the end of the tunnel. It was a sure enough formula, except he knew the truth and that was he was a mediocre priest but a virtuoso of death. On nights like this when he saw the faces of his victims, he would turn to drink and wallow at a local bar every time the ghosts came knocking on the doors of his conscience.

"Crush!" He turned to investigate the noise behind him, as alert and ready to act as the soldier he once was. A waiter had tripped and dropped his tray full of empty glasses, causing a loud, disruptive noise.

As soon as he realised there was no cause for alarm, he turned back to his drink, taking a huge gulp of the golden-brown elixir as if compensating for the wasted precious drinking time it took for him to investigate the scene behind him. He tried to move on and ordered another drink but his psyche was a house of cards after what he had been through. The sound of glass shattering triggered a painful recurring memory that still haunted his days. Years passed and after treatment by two therapists, his thoughts ran wild in flashback memory as he waited for his drink.

He was dropped off in an orphanage at the tender age of three. He couldn't quite remember the face of the lady presumed biological mother who very cliché-like dropped him off in a basket at the front door porch of the orphanage he would call home. In fact, he didn't remember much of her apart from the smell of her dark hair. She smelled of lavender and roses.

With no direct family, naturally he put a romanticised value on friendship, and as fate would have it in the very orphanage, he was left to rot in. He made a friend to whom his fate and future from troubled youth to soldier, to priest, and the glorious unknown would forever be intertwined.

He grew up with Nathan in the humble abode where the neighbourhood like the city then and now more than ever was a territory subject to turf wars between the Russian mob and the Italian mafia.

On the commute to and from school, they would run into crime scenes secured by the iconic 'do-not-cross' yellow tape the police usually placed around active crime scenes. The puddles of blood and bodies covered in white sheets that they would casually come across while growing up enforced in them the notion of the wages of crime and its notoriety of how unrewarding it eventually was at a very impressionable age. One would argue that it was that very same notion that set them on a path of joining the marines where they would become the finest soldiers in their class as opposed to choosing the path of least resistance and getting involved with the organised crime factions in their immediate environment.

The Italian mafia were particularly ruthless. They had a saying, *"Una vita per una vita,"* a mantra used to inspire vengeance, "A life for a life." For anyone taken from their ranks, they would avenge accordingly. The saying became hugely popular and heavily associated with the murder rate in the city at the peak of the turf war between the rival factions.

Dionysus showed aptitude for marksmanship while Nathan worked with explosives, and just as luck would have it, they ended up working in the same unit together until the height of both their careers, Dionysus, a world-class sniper and Nathan, an explosives and demolition expert.

There were a few close calls and life-threatening situations but they would both come out unscathed in all missions. Not until one fateful afternoon in the Middle Eastern desert, Nathan's unit was about to breach a compound occupied by assailants. Dionysus, being the sniper, was perched on a tree, camouflaged to match the colour of the leaves with an aerial advantage and clear field of view.

Ideally, snipers need spotters, a person to accompany them with a scoped device to determine oblique winds' range and degrees on which to adjust the scope to hit the targets but he was an excellent marksman with a record-breaking body count and preferred to be alone when pulling the trigger.

His task was to provide cover for his team from a distance as they breached the compound. He liquidated all the threats with exempt of women and children who watched in disbelief as the terrorist and terrorist-affiliated men based in the compound fell to their deaths from deadly headshots from his 'S Heckler & Koch M110A1 sniper rifle.' "Targets neutralised slingshot over," he spoke on his communications device that was inserted in his left ear as it blast out static noise before a voice responded,

"Copy that slingshot." As the team was securing the compound, all threats being neutralised as per Dionysus, a boy who couldn't have been older than ten years old, picked up a rifle that was on the ground next to the body of his slain father and aimed it at Nathan. A conflicted Dionysus saw it all happen from a distance but hesitated to pull his trigger as anyone with a conscience would.

The rapid burst of fire of bullets hailed towards Nathan from the boy's rifle made a thud as they pierced Nathan's torso. Dionysus watched helplessly as his oldest friend dropped dead from the gunshots, all while birthing his defining moment.

He remembered a certain Italian saying popular in the town he grew up in. "Una vita per una vita," and in a rash moment of temporary insanity, he aimed his rifle at the boy's head and took his life, saving the rest of the team that might have met the same fate had he not intervened and thus the infamous turn on the trail, the proverbial tipping point that brought him to his knees in a very conflicting turn of events.

In the spirit of dark clouds and their individual silver linings, he received a military commendation and was awarded the Purple Heart Medal for acts of valour at the cost of his soul and an old friend he considered a brother.

He soon after donated all his earnings from his years of service in the military to the orphanage that he and Nathan grew up and joined the church where he later became a priest and would drink like a docked sailor at the 'Moon Crystal' Bar and restaurant which was close to his accommodations whenever the ghost of wars' past came calling.

"Here's your drink, *padre*," the bartender said to Father Dionysus, interrupting his flashback on his defining moment.

"Thank you, young man," he responded. It was an anomaly that he and Genevieve had never met. He turned around to see who was behind him in the nearly empty bar. As it was getting late, he saw a couple four tables down that seemed about ready to ask for the bill, some out-of-town businessmen smoking cigars and presumably blowing off steam, and a few tables besides them was the most beautiful woman he had ever laid eyes on. Dionysus and Genevieve shared eye-contact briefly before he timidly turned away and continued sipping his drink, all the while thinking to himself what a vision she was.

"Forgive me, Father, for I have sinned," a feminine voice jokingly said as he quickly turned to find Genevieve away from her table and standing fairly close to his barstool, invading his personal space. She smelled like roses and lavender mixed with a day's work sweat. He found the scent very arousing. She giggled and added, "May I join you? It's no fun drinking alone."

"Please do," he responded as she pulled up a barstool and sat next to him. "Father Dionysus." He extended his arm for a handshake.

"Genevieve Henrietta." She did the same.

"So, Dionysus, is it okay if I skip the Father part and just call you Dionysus? Forgive my lapse of decorum but this seems like hardly the place to call you by your full title," she continued, being as charming and straightforward as she was known to be.

"I guess, given the circumstances, that would be appropriate," he responded, surprised by how bold and well-spoken she was.

"I know my reasons for being here tonight are more celebratory as opposed to the wallow and drink combination you seem to be on at the moment. I typically wouldn't approach men but a priest at a bar binge-drinking bourbon is too much of a mystery for me to pass up." They both laughed as he reached for his priest collar and put it in his pocket.

"I wasn't always a priest." His remark was a common response with men in his field, its objective being to humanise them.

"What's the purpose for celebration?" he asked.

"I just had the most industrious day of my career. I will not bore you with the details but it's significant."

"Congratulations," he responded with a genuine smile as she looked back at him with contentment that he would forget his woes even for a slight second to give a stranger a smile and a positive reaction to her good fortune was well received by her.

"Dare I ask your purpose of sulking at a bar?" she asked cautiously, not to seem pushy at getting information out of him.

"Like I said I wasn't always a priest. I was a soldier before this."

The vexed look on her facade was a familiar sight to him, a common facial expression on everyone he told his past to. "Every now and then, the ghosts and memories come flooding in and I attempt while failing miserably to drown them in bourbon… However, that doesn't stop me from trying," he responded as he signalled the waiter for another round of bourbon and whatever she was having.

"Corpse reviver," she told the bartender her cocktail order and quickly looked back to lock eyes with Dionysus.

They talked about politics and their mutual abhor for the current organised crime nuisance in the city. They exchanged world views and personal philosophy, all while enjoying each other's wit and charm throughout the odd hours of the night, unaware of how they would eventually play crucial roles in each other's lives down to the very end, a flame-engulfed blaze of scorched earth, ruin, and murder!

"We close in ten minutes," the bartender addressed them subtly, letting them know that they had to vacate the premises. Dionysus asked for the combined bill and gave a generous tip as they sipped on what was left of their drinks before heading out. He walked her to her car where her driver was waiting.

"This has been quite the unexpected yet refreshingly pleasant evening," she said while giving him a lusty look. There was something about corrupting a man of the cloth that she found extremely erotic. However, she had a strong insight that he was a man of content with a unique skillset and would somehow serve her ambitions in the near future. She desired him but did not want to risk losing a likeminded potential comrade over the temporary pursuits of meaningless intoxicating sex.

"I couldn't agree more," he reciprocated her discreet compliment as he primed himself for a conclusion to the evening and unexpected encounter. "I am at the Saint Paul's Church just down the street. Maybe we could finish that confession you were about to give at the bar," he added as they both laughed and parted ways, her in her driven town car and him through a dark alley.

Chapter IV
Mr. Mayor! Mr. Mayor!

Patrick walked through the lobby of the grand hall where he was about to hold a press conference to address the recent crime-rate spike. An entire week had passed since his passionate encounter with Genevieve. Being the mayor of the city naturally meant that he had a lot on his plate. Yet, she dominated his hourly thoughts and he was at the precipice of obsession as he had unknowingly imprinted on her like a cub to its mother.

He thought of her more than he did his wife and children, the floral scent of her hair lingering as if she was right next to him in the room, the sensation of her lips on his, and the warmth and taste of her silky skin to the sudden turn of her eyes to a demon serpent-like yellow with inverted pupils snapping him out of his daydreams, of which he interpreted as his guilty conscience purging impure thoughts by turning the object of his adulterated desire into a frightful entity, unaware that he was in fact recalling actual chain of events.

The thought of her would eventually consume his mind like a slow demented yet erotic dementia, as that was the power of her sway or curse opinion based on perception.

Genevieve deemed it the 'omnibus homines,' meaning, 'all men.' It had been the root cause of many a downfall of kings and kingdoms over time and she paid the ultimate price to be able to wield it.

He walked to the set-up podium, collected his thoughts, and began to address the members of press who were looking at him, eagerly waiting for him to finish the formalities so they could ask their pressing questions. "Good morning, ladies and gentlemen. Today's press conference's objective is to formally address the concern of a citywide crime-rate inflation over the last five years." He realised he would save more time if he got straight to the heart of the matter and confront the purpose of the gathering rather than showing off his charm and political prowess to aid his public approval.

"It's no secret that our beautiful city is plagued with a crime pestilence. It is also well known that the hard-working men and women earning an honest living are the pillars of this community and that gives me hope as it should to those good people. It gives me hope that we shall overcome organised crime and the deathly grip it's had on this city for too long. The crime rate and corruption is at its height. Tax-paying citizens turn on the news to see reports of senseless murders and indictments on corrupt elected city officials. It's a true mess, one that comes at the cost of the innocent and I'm here to assure you that the winds of change have caught on. I, as mayor, working together with local law enforcement, have put together an elite task force to put an end to this nightmare and to set this great city on the course it should be."

Genevieve watched the mayor's speech from the television in her living room as she ate her breakfast, preparing to head out for the day.

"To conclude this press release, I have some good news." The reporters all grabbed their notepads, recording devices, and assorted tools of the trade, hanging from his every word and ready to record the much-awaited punch line to his very inspiring speech.

"I have spearheaded a contract with one of the most established development firms in the world, the FIRST FRUIT CORPORATION, to give the city a full refurbishment, making it a global architectural marvel and leading authority on development and infrastructure." Genevieve rivalled at her seamless victory as the mayor announced the contract on live television. The bell had been rung and there was no turning back.

"Mr. Mayor! Mr. Mayor!" they shouted for his attention, hoping he would select the loudest and most frantic of the lot for a tip in the press conference now turned QNA but there was no bias or working formula. He randomly selected the reporters of his choice and the questions began flowing in. Genevieve texted her assistant, Jessica, asking her to inform the board members that the mayor was talking about their recently acquired contract on live television and they should tune in.

"Mr. Mayor, why did FFC get the contract?" one reporter boldly asked, leaving Genevieve in a complete anxious mess to what his answer would be. The omnibus hominess spell had never failed her before but she wasn't going to have the mayor publicly blubber about how he got swayed by a sex demon with serpent eyes to give the contract to the company, as that would make the public doubt his mental health status, voiding all executive decisions made from his office of power.

"That is a great question." Genevieve held her breath at the uncertainty of what his accompanying words would be. "They are a team of very talented architects and engineers led by the very impressive Miss Genevieve Henrietta who has done wonders in the development sector and needs no introduction. Next question." His answer gave her great relief as well as accents of guilt. Her sway would eventually rob him of his mind once her will was done. The spell had nothing to do with the answer he gave and she realised that she had doomed a person who genuinely held her in the highest regard. She told herself that he was a casualty of her ambition and got back to her normal guilt-free natural self in a bat of an eyelid as she stared at the television set, awaiting the next question from the unexpectedly intuitive line-up of reporters.

"Mr. Mayor! Mr. Mayor!" they shouted individually for his attention and what came out as a result was a collective of inaudible noise, unbearable and drowning the room. He hastily selected the reporter of his choice by pointing at her to put an end to the disruptive racket. "Mr. Mayor, Jacklyn Serabona, the Citizen Times Paper," she introduced herself and her place of employment, a formality the previous reporter skipped. He found her professional ethic refreshing and could tell right away that her question would be detailed and challenging to answer but he had already selected his pick out of the litter and there were no take-backs. "Given your initiative to overlook both the organised crime reform and infrastructure of the city, are you concerned that one will cause obstacles for the other and possibly cause retaliation from the mob which has allegedly been embedded in the city's dark financial and economic apparatus for decades?"

Genevieve's heart skipped a beat at the question as she grabbed the remote and turned up the volume on her television set. She prided herself on being the most informed person in any room but wasn't fully aware of how deep the mob ties in the city ran. The intuitive reporter's question gave her some sort of perception on the matter as she started to realise an unforeseen problem for her development ambitions in the citywide mafia territory, as she had no affiliations or associations with the criminal underworld. The larger spectrum was clear to her and she understood the cause of Patrick's initial reluctance on her citywide infrastructural proposal before she put her charms on him.

"What did you say your name was?" he asked her, surprised and both impressed by how bold and confrontational her question was.

"Jacklyn Serabona, Citizen Times," she replied, again mentioning her place of employment as if pivoting where she could easily be found on a daily basis, either that or shameless brand promoting.

"Well, Miss Jacklyn, you ask a difficult question, one that I don't have an answer to yet, as both initiatives have only just been set in motion. The law has a very long reach and justice shall not be hindered. Thank you. That will be all." His diplomatic answer left the journalists in the room wanting and unsatisfied from its vague and borderline cryptic nature.

"Mr. Mayor! Mr. Mayor!" They were even louder the second time around, as Jacklyn had exposed a weak point and the hounds of media had gotten an insatiable taste for blood. They would not relent and he would not let up as they followed him, shouting, "Mr. Mayor! Mr. Mayor!" at his parked motorcade outside the grand hall, the only thing standing between him and the bickering crowd being his security detail.

He made it to his car and got in. "Where to, Mr. Mayor?" the driver asked as he pushed the central locking mechanism button, locking all the doors in the car. He took a moment to respond as he debated in his mind whether or not it was the appropriate hour for lunch and the lingering thought on what colour of lingerie Genevieve was wearing to work. He fancied burgundy. "Mr. Mayor?" the driver asked, pulling him out of his thoughts, hoping to reinforce the initial question on where he would like to be driven to.

"Moon Crystal Bar and Restaurant. I'm famished."

"Certainly, sir," the driver responded as he put the car in gear, priming it for take-off, his security detail in a car behind them hot on their trail as they drove off.

They pulled up to the driveway where the owner of the establishment, Giani Moretti, was eagerly waiting for his arrival. His security detail took the liberty of calling ahead and letting him know that the mayor would be joining him for lunch in his restaurant, as was custom whenever he decided to visit them for a sitting.

The driver opened the door and he stepped out. *"Ay ciao bello."* The mayor quickly extended his arm to greet his. They shook hands as they made their way into an empty section of the restaurant and sat. "Bring us the 1975 Brunello Monti and then give us *un momento di privacy,"* he instructed the waiter who was eagerly awaiting instructions.

On the table was his mahogany finished cigar humidor ashtrays and some wine glasses. The waiter brought the wine to the table. "*Il vino che hai selezionato,* the wine you selected." He said it in both Italian and English for Giani's sake, as Italian was the language he was most comfortable with in informal conversation. It reminded him of Sicily, the city he grew up in. *"Si,"* he responded, nodding and giving him his approval to go ahead and open and serve the costly elixir, of which he did and hastily left the section, giving them a moment of privacy as Giani had requested.

He reached for his humidor and pulled out two cigars from his neatly piled, well-stocked cigar box and handed one to Patrick. "I had these flown in from Sicily last night," he added subtly, letting him know that he spared no expense in hosting him.

"Grazzi mille," Patrick responded as he reached for the smoking paraphernalia on the table, a golden cigar-cutter and a silver methane lighter with oaken accents. He snipped one end of torpedo-shaped cigar with the cutter and lit the other end using the lighter. The blue flames snapped and cracked as it caught a blaze and he put it in his mouth, taking puffs that instantly gave out huge clouds of smoke.

"I saw your press conference this morning and I have to say it was very bold, reckless but bold nonetheless. Explain yourself." Giani leaned in to his table, leaving an inappropriate distance between himself and the mayor, an intimidation tactic that bore results particularly with those who knew him well. Giani Moretti was a respectable businessman to the naked eye but on the same token the head of the Moretti Mob family that had allegedly ruled the criminal underworld in the city for two decades.

He was handed the reins after the brutal assassination of his predecessor, one that he could easily be presumed to be responsible for if the concept of *que bono* is at play, seeing as how twenty years ago a crafty placed car bomb went off outside his restaurant, the now-named Moon Crystal and formally named Moretti's Bar and Restaurant, a well-known favourite wine and dining establishment for the mob taking out his predecessor and his heirs, making him the youngest and most brutal leader to emerge from the murk.

"Giani…" Patrick was interrupted before he could utter his name and immediately corrected on his lapse in decorum.

"It's Don Giani to you." He viciously reminded the mayor the manner of how to address him.

"Don Giani, it was a ploy." His voice trembled as he tried to explain his motives on declaring his citywide organised crime takedown rhetoric and infrastructure development initiative he publicly announced in his press conference without as much as giving those he was in cahoots with a courtesy call. He was clearly answerable to the don. The mayor of Clarence City was but a glorified henchman for the Moretti family, as were many city officials.

He typically wouldn't do something so counter-self-preservative but Genevieve's spell had rendered many a great men to make foolish, inadvisable moves, seeing as those who crossed the Moretti family had a poisson of meeting an untimely demise, either from untraceable poison-oriented assassinations which the coroner would deem as a sudden heart attack for lack of evidence to declare foul play or the more subtle and his personal favourite means of getting rid of a problem, demise by fatal 'accident,' as no one would investigate death from a broken neck caused by a fall from a flight of stairs.

Every so often, he would be required to send a message to his rivals and the victims of his wrath would end up on the coroner's table, deceased from a term his underboss causally titled as 'lead poisoning' from eating the abundant bullets they would 'serve' and would not sit well with their target's digestive system, not to forget the occasional car bomb for multiple casualties. Don Giani was truly an agent of the macabre and Patrick, the mayor, was walking on a hypothetical tight rope, of which his successful cross to safety would be based on how he explained his recent choices and his plunder the equivalent of falling out of favour with Don Giani, making him the object of his wrath and an example to be made of if the don did not approve of his methods... "A ploy you say." Giani leaned back in his chair and took a huge puff from his cigar. "Explain," he continued.

"Don Giani, the days of organised crime in Clarence City are numbered. The newly elected president is on a warpath and has a personal vendetta of getting rid of the city's infamous crime families to spike his public approval ratings. It's high up on the agenda of tasks to complete within his first hundred days in office, and as the mayor, I have been receiving mandate after mandate to come up with a solution for the problem at hand. Who better to lead an investigation on the crime factions than myself? One who is deeply involved with and loyal to a fault to the Moretti family." Patrick concluded his pitch as if his life depended on it. It might as well have.

"What about the changes in infrastructure and the company that received the contract? You know well and good that the biggest asset for the Moretti family is infrastructure and real estate within city limits. By giving that random company the contract to change the city skyline, you have taken money from the family's financial apparatus." The don spoke in a calm, non-threatening tone as he stated the facts on what the consequences of the mayor's actions would eventually be.

"Genevieve is a goddess among women," Patrick responded half-dazed and with a stupendous smile to pair his moronic answer.

"You declare war on my family! You take money and potential opportunities from my family! You, Mr. Mayor, are an enemy of the family." The don raised his voice to reinforce the dominance his presence usually brought about as well as making it clear to the mayor the severity of the matter at hand and its unhealthy consequences that would without a doubt leave the mayor with a serious case of lead poisoning. He sat there smiling back at the don as if he had temporarily lost his mind. Giani realised his efforts were in vain. He abruptly left the table before his patience wore out and he strangled the mayor with his bare hands in front of all the witnesses.

He walked away accompanied by four muscular gentlemen clad in Italian tailored suits who were spread out across the restaurant like interior-design ornaments. Don Giani needed to be as far away from the mayor as possible for the sake of his alibi. Patrick might have not been aware of it but he was marked for dead from the moment word publicly came out that he had given the contract to the First

Fruit Corporation. Giani and him had a long history of *quid pro quo* and he felt that regardless of his offence to the family, he did not deserve to go out in a hail of bullets. All he had to do was wait a few hours and the profusely ricin poison infused Sicilian flown in cigar he gave the mayor would kick in, stopping his heart and killing him in minutes.

Patrick snapped out of his omnibus trance and walked towards the exit where his security detail had the entourage ready. All he could think about was Genevieve despite feeling lightheaded. He assumed it was the wine and cigar combination he had as an early lunch. He fell to the ground seizing while attempting to bend over to enter his vehicle.

"Mr. Mayor! Mr. Mayor!" His security ran to his aid as he seized and convulsed. The ricin had taken its effect. They watched helplessly, shouting, "Mr. Mayor! Mr. Mayor!" as Patrick lay dead on the filthy parking lot.

Chapter V
Matsya Nyaya: 'Law of Fish'

Politicians, city officials, and civilians alike, all gathered at the grand hall steps to give the late beloved mayor of Clarence City the hero's send-off they were led to believe he deserved. On the ground where roses and a red carpet to pave the way for his Paul bearers to where the late Mayor's coffin would be displayed, officers of Scottish decent from the local precinct menagerie easily deduced from their aptitude for the bag pipe and the kilts they wore played a sad tune as they marched forward to the assembly line, as was routine when the city buried its top government officials. The news dominated by documentaries of his earlier life achievements replayed interviews and his final press conference where he made rhetoric to reform and rebuild the city, a task he left unattended from an untimely demise. The cause of death on the medical report was a heart attack but word to the wise… consequences of crossing the infamous Moretti family.

Huge parts of the city were inaccessible due to the masses gathered for the late mayor's funeral. Traffic was diverted and all those who did not join the send-off had to wait for hours in traffic as an alternative. Genevieve fell into the latter category of those who had to endure the brutal delay to get to their destinations.

She had scheduled for a board meeting. It was no secret that the mayor was a key player at giving FFC the contract to rebuild the city and with his passing, she needed to reassure the board that they were still on course. She knew the law well and was certain that whoever was to take over the reins from the late mayor had to finish his mandates and pending initiatives before bringing any new ideas of his or her own to the table a fact. She was going to enforce to her very anxious board members in order to calm them down.

A few cars ahead of hers was Don Giani's town limousine. They were both primarily responsible for Patrick's death, shared the same circles, and attended the same social functions. She even frequented the restaurant owned by the don. Yet, the fact that they had never met would make a hypothetical third-party entity looking at the chain of events, playing out like a narrator to a play or a chess master staring at his chessboard at full spectrum view, appreciating the irony, convincing even the biggest sceptic in fate, and its decision to deem their acquaintance premature until the destined moment.

He too had an important agenda and had summoned the heads of the four Italian families that answered to him to explain the changes that were to come. Unlike Genevieve, he was restless and extremely eager to get to his destination, yelling at the driver to find a solution to manoeuvre through the worst traffic the city had seen in ages.

With Patrick dead, he had lost his protection from persecution for him and his henchmen. The counterweights that tilted the scales of justice to his advantage were no more and after the late mayor's press conference where he swore to wage war on organised crime, the don desperately needed to regroup with his underlings of malice to plan on how they would cautiously operate from henceforth. He truly grasped the gravity of his predicament. He wasn't going to come out of his planned retreat until he had the upper hand and was confident his natural position at the top of the pyramid wasn't in jeopardy. He thought himself a megalodon of the ocean that is the criminal underworld, a predator who is prey to none.

She was certain that she was the root cause of Patrick's demise. Her omnibus curse always had the same end result. The men who were unfortunate enough to fall victim to it would go through certain stages of deterioration, the first being a state of dementia fuelled by erotic thoughts and fantasies of a life with Genevieve until eventually they would be unable to separate fantasy from reality. The second would be a catatonic state with a certain mortality rate. She felt no remorse for all those who fell under the spell and from her twisted logic. She considered herself as the physical manifestation of the wages of sin which was known to be death. Her mind started to wonder on the cruelty of men and how she came about the means to their end as the traffic moved at an unsettling pace of an inch an hour.

How times have changed, she thought to herself as she looked outside her car window to a skyline view of the city. If anyone would have told her younger self the engineering technological advancements that were to come in the future, she would have considered them mentally unfit. She grew up in a small village of fishermen based along shores of the intersection of four rivers where the changing of currents naturally meant it was the ideal habitat and feeding grounds for fish and a bountiful harvest for the fishermen. Taking lessons to hone the skills of their livelihood from her father, she mastered the rod but was particularly fond of the casting net that captured fish large and small alike, setting the smaller ones free for the next harvest or as prey to sustain larger fish.

The law of fish that states the bigger fish devours the smaller one was a lesson her father taught her that had real world applications and that came to her while the Carthaginian soldiers pillaged and plundered her village on their way to fight a roman legion that was advancing from the north. They slaughtered men, women, and children, including her family indiscriminately. The memory of the fateful siege of where she lost her raison d'être and soul hurt like a fresh wound. She couldn't pinpoint where exactly her village was to date, as time had taken its toll and the gulf sea had swallowed the entire landscape, leaving behind two rivers out of the four that intersected, flowing through Persia. Modern-day Iraq, if she could, she would go back to feed her nostalgia and to attempt to reconcile with her traumatic past of her, being the small fish in hopes of closure. Thus began her endeavour to be the biggest fish in any ocean and to never be the victim of the cruelty of men.

Chapter VI
The Cruelty of Men

Her fondest memory was the view to a small island that was almost completely submerged in water, leaving only a great oak tree at its tip that was visible for miles and appeared to be floating on water as a horizon optic illusion in the middle of the intersection. This was the same tree she had, a replica sculpted in the lobby of her skyscraper.

It was the beginning of the second Punic War unlike today's flow of information with the internet and social media keeping everyone informed about the day-to-day happenings. Information was constricted to a personal face-to-face engagement or manuscripts and letters, leaving only the parties involved aware of what transpired. Members of her village were oblivious of the war that was taking place. If they had been aware, they would have taken precautions to remove themselves from the path of either side of the conflict due to their pacifist nature.

The Romans who were known throughout history to be civil and the forefathers of democracy presumably would have asked for every able man in the village to join the fight as squire aids and battle infantry, compensating them for services rendered. She often wondered what would have happened if they instead of the Carthaginians found her settlement. Carthaginians, on the other hand, believed themselves to be on the righteous path of fighting tyranny and thought deliverance from Roman rule of the local tribes as a gift in its own self and anyone who denied to join their ranks for whatever reason was pledging loyalty to the Roman oppressors and was an enemy deserving of a swift death, as was the fate of her village when the chief, her father, turned down the general's proposition to join his cause and fight his war.

The village was swiftly taken by the formidable army, as they refused to take up arms, leading to a swift victory for the battalion and a meaningless slaughter for the tribesmen.

A group of soldiers bound her hands and tied her up to a nearby tree where she sat bound and was forced to watch her village burn. The corpse of her dismembered father lay a few paces away from his head that was mounted on a pike, as was the Carthaginian tradition and fate of the leaders of their enemies. Her siblings slain and corpses scattered over a stone-throw distance. She sobbed uncontrollably as she saw soldiers taking turns at raping a woman whose voice when she screamed was the voice of her own mother. Genevieve, who then went by the name Giaya, wailed and cried for the last time she would ever do so as the soldiers drove a sword in her mother's torso, taking her will to live when they were done, leaving her lifeless impaled corpse on the ground, laughing as they continued to scavenge for spoils of war.

She wondered why she was spared and craved for death, a coup de grâce to spare her from her anguish. "Spoils for the general," she overheard one of the soldiers tell his comrades as he shamelessly pointed at her. The worst had been done to her. She had witnessed the death of her family and was certain no more pain and suffering could possibly be caused to her. Her spirit died as she processed what had transpired.

When the smoke had cleared, the soldiers slept off the weariness of pillage and plunder. She closed her eyes not to rest but to fantasise death and to pray to her deities and forces that may be to exert terrible vengeance on the evil men that might as well have ripped her beating heart out of her chest from the grief caused.

As she closed her eyes and hoped to never open them again, it was then she had a vision. She was clad in a white dress in an open space of the darkest shade of black. The floor covered with fairly three inches of dark semi-liquid ooze that submerged her bare feet until her ankles, moulding and quickly covering up her footprints as she followed the light breeze that brushed on her bare shoulders from the east.

A glimmering light hit from above and was instantly absorbed by the absolute black. Beneath it, in a shiny silhouette fashion, was a tall man clad in white robes. She found his facial symmetry uniquely appealing and his physique to be godlike. She could pick up his musk of smoke and firewood with hints of a strong burned sage from where she stood. "Who are you?" she asked, making her way towards him, puzzled by the direction her very vivid vision was heading. Her mind couldn't translate what was going on. It was as if her spirit had been projected to the great unknown, to a hall of pitch darkness and nothingness without doors or windows, just an audience with a tall, handsome man in white robes stained from his knee down by the same dark ooze that was evenly spread on the floor.

"I could sense your anguish, your pain, and most delicious hate," he responded in the deepest voice she had ever heard a man speak in. She often compared it to the slight after-rumble of fading thunder. "I offer you the power to respond to the cruelty of men with an even deeper unfathomable cruelty delivered by your hand in my service for as long as men are still cruel… at the measly price of your soul, mine to keep and your will shall be mine, my bidding your will." His proposition was well thought of, as the great deceiver only made deals when certain he would not be rejected.

Every fibre of her being told her to neglect the offer and that she was in the presence of pure malice but her anger and grief clouded her judgment and she would have gladly paid whatever cost to be personally responsible for exacting vengeance on the soldiers that took everything from her.

"I accept your proposition," she uttered the words of her damnation, oblivious to their consequences like a baby in the bush.

During the entire encounter, the man showed no emotion, just a stern look until she uttered the words of her acceptance that were soon followed by an embrace to seal the deal. He smiled for the first time since she met him, looking at his face while locked in an embrace. She noticed the black of his eyes had turned into a reptilian yellow with vertical pupils, and just before she could address the terrifying phenomena, he vanished into a thick cloud of smoke that left behind burning debris of sparky ashes floating in the air and falling to the ground in a seesaw pattern, like a feather dropped from arm's-length height. Her hands drenched in a terrible residue of dark slimy ooze, and before she could soak in what had happened, she winced from a piercing pain on her right foot and was snapped back to reality before she could look down to see what caused the excruciating pain.

She woke bound and even more heartbroken than she was earlier. The smell of war and burning flesh strong in the air and on the ground where the soldiers lay at spitting distance from the soles of her feet was the biggest serpent she had ever seen. It had a head the size of a rock and was of pure white colour. She did not bother to ask for help and remained strangely composed, given the circumstances. She would have considered death by venomous bite on her darkest day as a kindness and relief from what she had endured. It slithered closer and coiled its massive head back as if priming for a strike.

Never had she seen such an enormous serpent. She thought it supernatural and fully capable of swallowing her whole, gawking at it in contempt and with a certain acceptance of her fate until she recognised its bright yellow serpent eyes, the same shade and shape as those of the man from her vision. She looked at her right foot and just beneath the puncture wounds from the bite was an infinity symbol, branded onto to her skin in dark ink like a medieval tribe tattoo that she did not have before the mysterious encounter. Convulsing as the venom kicked in, she heard in her head the terrifying voice of the tall man in white robes repeatedly chanting a phrase in Latin, *"Ante omnem infirmitatem. Amte omnem infirmitatem,"* over and over as the serpent hissed continuously, a trait modern-day animal experts would classify as an intimidation tactic to perceived threats. However, this was no regular serpent but a vessel possessed by the deceiver of men, the entity from her vision. It hissed, expelling a breath of evil from its insides as if a demented hurrah celebrating her death and her dark rebirth. The serpent slithered away into the river on an apparent course for the tree on the submerged island in the centre of the intersecting river as the sun began to rise and she came to consciousness.

Gasping for precious air like a resuscitated man brought back from the jaws of death, she opened her eyes and hoped it was all a bad dream but her village was still on fire, her family dead, and the infinity-symbol tattoo on her intact, peculiarly not even slightly sore, as if she had it for ages.

The soldiers awoke and prepared to gather themselves for the march line-up to their next destination, eventually leading to a head-on battle with a roman legion tasked to put an end to the Carthaginian sacred band that would certainly make its way to the steps of Rome if not confronted.

The general advanced towards her. He was of medium build and had a darker complexion that she assumed was caused by the heat in Carthage. He got down on his knees to unbind her tethers. "Did they hurt you?" he asked.

She gave him a cynical look. "You kill my kin, burn my village, and worry if your men that you instructed to kill and pillage caused me harm?" she asked bitterly and full of resentment to his false concern about her wellbeing.

"War is a terrible thing. Yet necessary, I offered your father a choice to join my cause as the other tribes we ran into have and like the ones we will encounter will but he refused to take up arms against the Roman oppressors and sealed his fate and unfortunately that of his village." A hate of unimaginable passion overcame her on hearing his motives for slaughtering her kin and tribesmen.

What a terrible person he must be to order the massacre of innocence to ease his challenged ego! she thought.

"What do they call you?" he asked.

"Giaya," she responded.

"My name is General Hannibal Barca and I claim you as my spoil of war. You are now under my care and protection rise, for you are now, Giaya, citizen of Carthage," he spoke loudly, announcing his claim to her and his approval to her coronation to one of their own as he helped her to her feet and handed her to his female squires who would bath her and dress fit to be his concubine.

BEEP! the hooting in unison as the roads cleared pulled Genevieve out of her rumination and back to reality. The funeral march had moved to the west side of the city as they made their way to the cemetery. Her driver knew how to manoeuvre the city well, and she was at the driveway to her building shortly after. As was routine, the valet held the car's door open for her and she stepped out, giving him a glimpse of her infinity-symbol tattoo on her right foot while exiting the vehicle.

She made her way, as was the norm to the massive feature in the lobby of the sculpture of the tree on the tip of the submerged island in the middle of intersecting rivers and a huge serpent curled up in its brunches where she took a moment to look at it before engaging in any other work-related entanglements.

There was something about this morning that she couldn't shake. She had a vivid memory she hadn't had in ages, one of her dark rebirth and of her time as a concubine for one the greatest generals to have ever lived, General Hannibal Barca, the man who would eventually become a victim of her omen omnibus spell, leading to the fall of Carthage.

She snapped out her daze and made her way to the board to address her board members and to lay down an action plan on how they would go about their ambitions to rebuild the city skyline, given that they had lost the mayor their foremost advocate to their infrastructural ambitions.

Chapter VII
The Devil in the Details

Her assistant, Jessica, was waiting for her by the elevator door, a hot beverage from her favourite restaurant in hand, as was the routine. "Good morning, Miss Henrietta?" she greeted her, not expecting a response, as it had been a long commute and they had a late start to a very busy day. Yet, she looked back at her and nodded an effortless salutation from Genevieve's part but a salutation nonetheless and she was flattered that she even got a response.

"John got a head start at addressing the board and collecting queries. I managed to overhear some of the concerns they brought up while you were making your way to work." She walked at the same pace as Genevieve, briefing her so she could be at per with the board members as much as possible when arriving to the meeting.

She opened the door to find all members present despite the mobility hurdles caused by the funeral. John had taken a sit-in at her usual spot, the CEO's chair, as the rest sat facing him on the typically designed boardroom table. He stood up to make way for her to claim her natural position and sit at the table. "I apologise for the delay. We all know what was going on this morning. It was the funeral of our late beloved mayor who not only did great things for the city including giving us a government contract to refurbish it to our state-of-the-art standards, but also he was a frequent esteemed guest at our board gatherings, as he had vetted interests of procuring shares to join our highly professional team, an ambition he will unfortunately not come to see. May he rest in peace!" Her remark was intuitive and straight to the heart of the matter.

"May he rest in peace!" the board responded in unison.

"Before you all voice your individual concerns, I would like to address the main purpose of this gathering and that is to reassure you all that we are still on course. Our constitution states that whatever initiatives or mandates began by any high-ranking government official must be completed even upon death by his successor. I made the necessary calls to the people concerned and I'm glad to announce that we are still having a go on our endeavours." The board members clapped and cheered at the news. She had answered all the pressing queries with an opening remark, thanks to the discreet pre-work brief her assistant, Jessica, gave her. She knew the pressure points and matters to address, making her appear impressively intuitive to her colleagues.

"Don't celebrate just yet." They held their applause that was drowning the room, turning it to a vacuum of silence as they sat on the edge of their seats, awaiting the other shoe to drop in form of the unforeseen obstacle Genevieve was about to point out. "Our plans look excellent and easily achievable on paper. We have the labour. We have the resources. God knows we have the skillset and expertise. However, what we did not account for was the human factor.

By that, I mean the displaced occupants in buildings we plan on renovating and the organised crime factions and their territories which happen to be on the same turf we plan on putting up skyscrapers and state-of-the-art townhouse apartments."

The board members shared looks of concern as it dawned on them how threatening to their collective and individual goals the blind spot Genevieve pointed out was. "I suggest we pay off the parties concerned," one board member said.

"Then we will never stop paying people off and word will come out that we played ball with the mob to achieve our plans. That will certainly taint the glory and significance of our current and future achievements," John, the most well-spoken man in the room, bluntly countered the preposterous proposition, his brilliance making him subject to the passive aggression of some of the members.

"Then what do you suggest?" another board member patronisingly asked John, hoping his words would choke him or even better yet, render his suggestion to be completely moronic.

"I suggest a discreet meeting with the heads of the crime families involved, of which we will discuss terms on how both parties remain satisfied." His answer pulled awe from the people present in the room as they whispered among themselves about how dangerous and counterintuitive his proposition to find common ground with the mob was. All but one Genevieve remained quiet as the rest went at one another, some using the debate to settle scores by snide comments, others bluntly insulting one another as tempers rose in the cause of finding a solution.

"I like it," she spoke and gave a moment for the flames of the heated argument to be extinguished by word of her approval. The room soon went quiet, its occupants intrigued to hear her motives for favouring John's proposition on their course of action. She added, "I understand your fear. John's idea requires us to expose our neck to the deadly blow of public humiliation. Yet, we forget that the city has been under the dark cloud of organised crime since I can remember… I see no other way to accomplish our goals. It is simply not feasible for the law enforcement apparatus tasked to put an end to the organised crime factions that have expanded their reach for decades in a matter of months. Waiting is clearly not an option, and if we decide to proceed construction on mafia territory without their seal of approval, they can seriously derail our progress by malicious damage to property or injuring even murdering the workers who are not susceptible to their intimidation tactics and continue to show up for work.

"The path of least resistance and the best chance we have on meeting the construction deadlines requires us to parlay with the mob." The room pondered on the sensible argument made by Genevieve and put it to a vote where they unanimously came to a landslide decision in favour of the motion that might as well have been translated to board agrees on making a deal with the devil on the minutes' conclusion that Jessica was taking.

"Can you set it up?" She looked into John's eyes with a look you would give a naughty toddler who thought had gotten away with stealing cookies from a jar and he looked back at hers, curious as to why she would specifically ask him to set up a meeting with the top brass of the criminal underworld.

"How could she possibly know? I made every effort to change my second name and even disown my family to get away from their murderous and criminal tendencies and reputation."

"Well?" she asked, interrupting his train of thoughts. "I can ask around." He gave a cryptic and vague answer that yet inspired confidence. He was truly hands-on and had a repertoire of great competence. He wondered if she was fully aware of his past, of which the only way to have done so would be to have him thoroughly investigated. He then shunned his thoughts and proclaimed them as paranoia, opting for the alternative and more likely idea that she trusted him to get the most challenging task done.

The meeting soon concluded and the board was dismissed as he made his way to their forty thousand square ft. family estate and the ideal place for his Uncle Don Giani to hide out. Don Giani had secretly summoned everyone under his domain, mob bosses and relatives alike. He thought about the unforeseen loopholes with Genevieve's and the FFC's ambitions to rebuild an entire city. He swore to be more vigilant, as his lack of foresight sent him to the one place he swore he would never return. Back on the bargaining table with his uncle and the mob, as he approached the Moretti estate, he pulled out a piece of paper and a red pen. He drew a sketch of a bus, the back matching the front, making it impossible to tell which direction the bus was moving to.

They were soon at the estate, as it was just within city limits, a well sought-after piece of prime real estate. As the chauffeur opened his door to let the prodigal son loose at his family, he could smell his grandmother's cooking, the overwhelming smell of oregano and basil leaves, and the muffled giggling and yelling of children playing coming from the house despite the door being locked. Even the rushing sound of running water could not conceal the inaudible background noise as he stood in front of the water feature, his chauffeur right behind him as if about to assist him with his luggage. However, he did not bring any, nor was he planning to stay, and had he not desperately needed to come to an arrangement for the sake of the FFC, he would not be looking at the palace housing the king of crime in Clarence City. He decided to take a minute before entering the house to gather himself, pulling out the sketch and handing it to his chauffeur. "Which direction is the bus heading?"

His chauffeur looked and could not answer. He tried to speculate on the lean of the drawing suggesting that downward force and gravity would ideally make a car in motion tilt towards the opposite direction of its trajectory but his answer was wrong. "For the life of me, I can't figure it out, sir." He accepted defeat and eagerly awaited an explanation from John.

"Where are the doors?" he asked the chauffeur, pointing out something of great significance he had not noticed on the drawing. "The passenger door is on the other side, therefore can't be seen on the drawing, suggesting that the bus is traveling forward from right to left!"

"Splendid, sir!" he responded as he laughed hysterically. They both laughed but for different reasons. His chauffeur found humour in the unexpected turn of events, but John found amusement in his chauffeur's luck of attention to detail, laughing until he suddenly stopped joining him in laughter and ominously said, "Never forget the devil is in the detail," as he made his way to the porch and gradually the door where he rang the bell and nervously awaited to be let in.

His gut that told him to turn back and to never return, clashed with his massive intellect that had run a risk reward analysis, suggesting that the spoils of bargain with the family outweighed the risks. The reward being finding a peaceful solution even as much as aid to endeavour from the mob to the First Fruit Corporation, the risk being re-inducted to the fold to be groomed and to eventually claim his birth right as heir to the bloody throne in the position of Don upon Don Giani's retirement or his death. In a world as violent as that of the mafia and organised crime, it would not be farfetched if one made an educated assumption that it would be the latter.

The door opened and a little girl in a polka-dot dress and a red ribbon tied on her head stood in front of him and stared in awe. "Mommy! Mommy! It's Uncle John from the pictures." Her mother, his Sister Stefania Moretti, at the time was carrying a bowl of pasta fazool that she dropped in utter shock on seeing the unexpected guest. He crossed the threshold and pushed the door, locking it behind him while his chauffeur watched from afar, unaware that John shutting the door as soon as he entered the house was more than just good bedside manners but rather symbolic of him leaving his innocence behind.

Chapter VIII
Crisis in Faith

Upon completion of the afternoon service, he looked at his watch, eagerly awaiting the appropriate time to make his leave to the bar for the afternoon beverages he was accustomed to consume on such peculiar evenings filled by dark thoughts of his previous occupation, particularly peculiar that it was one of those proverbial days of open flood gates to a cesspool of negative flashbacks that replayed and bargained between hindsight and probability.

Despite being denied peace of mind and a good night's sleep by his guilty conscience that was as menacing as a shark fin advancing towards swimmers in the ocean on a summer's day, he gave a wonderful summon on how good begets good and evil, its own, inspiring his congregation to be kind to each other and be the best version of themselves.

He then finished on a high note that left the congregation with food for thought to keep them engaged until they would gather next. "To the men of God in the room, never forget that every woman that sheds a tear for you is an invite of misfortune in your life brought upon by your own hand, for hell hath no fury like a woman scorned and closest to heaven it shall be if she is pleased." Father Dionysus concluded his sermon and made his way to the confession booth, as was procedure.

Typically, members of his perish were not so kin on joining him in the confession booth. He had two working theories, the first being that the modern-day progressiveness and forward thinking may have been the root cause of why many practicing Catholics no longer went to confess their sins, as it was trendy and fashionable to bear them in public as if a demented version of the scarlet letter that brought admiration instead of public shame. Therefore, getting absolved in God's house meant giving away their sense of accomplishment in their collective celebration of misdeeds.

The second was that as time progresses, what is considered as a sin is a vague uncharted area and subject to nature, environment, or unbearable guilt. Still, he followed due process and sat for an hour in his confession booth after service for the few that still followed conventional Catholicism within his congregation and needed some spiritual guidance. He hoped someone would walk in, though he remained doubtful until he heard the curtains pushed open and closed behind his fully concealed partition.

"Forgive me, Father, for I have sinned," a feminine and familiar voice spoke through the small holes in the blinds. He could make out that it was indeed a woman of dark hair and fair skin. She smelled like roses and lavender mixed with a day's work sweat, an intoxicating scent that filled the ill-lit booth and immediately reminded him of his encounter with Genevieve at the bar. He had his suspicions it was her but could not be certain, since he had not spotted her among the congregation.

"Welcome, my child," he acknowledged her presence, letting her know he was paying attention and ready to give a listening ear for her to unload her burden.

"It has been quite a long time since my last confession," she proceeded before being interrupted by Dionysus.

"My child, you are required by Catholicism to give an exact timeframe. In the rare event that it has been so long since your last confession that you cannot remember the time lapse, you are required to give an estimated one for avoiding confession, for a long period of time is a sin to be absolved of as well."

She took a moment before responding. He thought she was processing what he had told her, but in fact she was weighing her options on whether to unburden her centuries' worth of misdeeds and encounters with the macabre and supernatural, not to mention the issue of her difficult-to-imagine yet as certain as taxes immortality or to spare his innocence and core beliefs by picking a recent arbitrary sin from a long list of arbitrary sins of fornication or manipulation as one to be absolved. She, however, craved to be truly seen by one bound by more than a gentleman's code but of oath to keep her secrets. Her need of sweet release made her opt for the latter rather than the first.

"Father, I assure you this confession is not one you will soon forget. I have two humble requests if I am to give you the privilege and crucible alike of hearing my sins. First is, I am unfathomably out of practice. Therefore, I ask to be subject to exemption to the rules of due process in confession. The second is a tall order but I ask that you humour me despite how unlikely my story is, that you keep an open mind and believe my narrative and should you remain unconvinced, I would appreciate it if you believed that I believe." The only lady he had ever met with such a way with words and intellect was Genevieve at the Moon Crystal Bar fairly two weeks ago. He was nearly certain it was her but the margin of assumption was too big a gap that could only to be closed by visual confirmation.

"Proceed, my child. What are your sins?" he asked, eager to get the confession started but craftily hiding his need to know.

"You don't have enough years left to listen to all of them." She giggled, a familiar sound to his ears, adding to the grand speculation in his head that Genevieve was the one behind the partition.

"Let's start with what bothers you the most. What scratches at your soul? Tell me of that sin." She was impressed by his intuition. She always had an appreciation for a surgeon's poised scalpel as opposed to a carpenter's bashful hammer.

"I have sinned abundantly. There is, however, no sin that scratches at my soul, for I... I'm afraid I traded mine to a dark entity for what appears to be immortality and a supernatural sway over men, a blessing at first but now a curse without a question." As articulate as she was known to be, she brought up the topics that were least believable to test his patience and tolerance based on his response to determine if he would humour her and listen to her narrative.

"If this is some sort of joke, I assure the house of the Lord is no place for such inappropriate humour but if you are true and you are indeed in need of spiritual guidance, I shall listen to your story, advice you accordingly, and absolve you of your sins, lying being one of them if found to be in conclusion." He responded shortly after carefully selecting his words, for he knew this would be a story of epic proportions, if true, or a case of the most active imagination and entertainment, if false. It was not the answer she was expecting. Yet, it made her doubtful and inspired confidence at the same time. It had been a while since she found a dancing partner of her wit, grit, and practitioner of the subtle art of diplomatic answers that led to more questions than answers. It was refreshing and it gave her the impression that she could bear all to him and that he would indulge her.

"You mentioned immortality, a thing many a men over millennia have obsessed over, some say to be in possession of. It would mean absolute wealth, to never age, to never fall ill, to leave throughout history, and you claim you came across it from a dark entity in exchange for your soul, succeeding where millions of kings, presidents, empires, and scientists have failed. Did I miss a thing?"

She ignored the hint of sarcasm in his voice. "You seem to be up to speed," she added.

"I have had many names over the years. Giaya was the one my mother gave me but I have had at least twenty-five… one for every lifetime. I grew up in a small fishing village camped over the shores between intersecting rivers that nearly engulfed a mysterious island, leaving only a great leafless oak at the peak visible from the village shores and appeared to be floating as an optic illusion located somewhere between modern-day Iraq and Iran.

"We were pacifists that never believed in violence or taking up arms to defend ourselves ironically. That was our death sentence and General Hannibal Barca and his

Carthaginian fleet of soldiers, our executioners as they came across our village and requested us to take up arms against their enemies, the Romans in the second Punic War.

"My father, the chief, denied Hannibal of Carthage, his request stating our pacifistic nature as reason of why. He in turn slaughtered everyone in the village aside from me, a young beautiful girl coming into womanhood. He would reserve me as his spoils of war where I would later be his favourite concubine… While my village burned, the soldier tied me to a tree close to the shore as they proceeded to make merriment and celebrate their victory of slaughter, since no one lifted a finger to fight them. It was then in my deep despair that I shut my eyes in hopes that I would never open them again. I assume my spirit astro projected to a dark realm that being the only logical explanation for it was too vivid to be a vision.

"In this vision, I was clad in a pure white dress in an open space of pure vacuum and darkness, yet could see my hands and outfit in afternoon's light. The floor was covered in a thick ooze fairly three inches thick that formed and deformed like slime as I walked on it, following the cold breeze on my shoulder, walking towards a tall, handsome man standing ceremoniously, waiting for me as if a groom in the altar and I the bride.

"He offered me the capability to exert terrible vengeance and the power to never fall victim to cruelty of men in exchange for my soul. I agreed to his terms, for I had a strong incline that he does not offer with likelihood of rejection, nor would he offer twice, leaving me with a sense of urgency that this would be my only chance of acquiring the means to avenge my slain family and villagers. We embraced and he vanished into a thick cloud of black smoke, leaving behind sparks and brittles of ash falling on the ground... I was woken to reality by a piercing pain on my right ankle to open my eyes and find myself still bound to the tree with my feet covered in the black ooze from my vision, an infinity-symbol tattoo on my right ankle with two hardly noticeable puncture wounds below it and the largest white serpent I have ever seen in all my years alive. It must have been thirty feet long and had a meter-long girth. Its pupils were vertical, suggesting it was venomous and the puncture wounds were clearly caused by a snake bite. I immediately figured that I wasn't long for this world as my heart started pounding as if attempting to break out of my ribcage. I started to seize as it hissed loudly as if threatened but if I didn't know any better, I would say it was celebrating my rebirth. I was woken approximately two hours later by the soldiers to find the snake gone. It probably slithered into the water on course to the submerging island. One of the soldiers who couldn't have been older than twenty said I was chanting a phrase in ancient Latin, which was strange to me, for I did not speak the language at the time.

"The general took me as his concubine and I travelled with him as he attempted to make his way to the heart of Rome. It wasn't until he tried to take me sexually against my will that I came to my gift... the fruits of my trade with the dark entity from my vision... He mounted on top of me, ripping off my attire as he was about ready to exercise his sexual deviance on me. I involuntary spoke the words in Latin that the soldier claimed I was chanting and shall not repeat to you, for you too might fall under my spell like

Hannibal did. He became extremely tranquil and lay on top of me without moving a muscle. I turned and laid him on his back on the bed to see if the gods had answered my prayers and spared me from him by taking his life, but alas! He was alive, just completely impressionable and susceptible to my will like a submissive to her slave and a subject to her queen… I requested him to take his life by his own dagger, but as he was undeniably about to drive the knife to his diaphragm, I ordered him to halt, as his men would not believe their conquering hero would take his own life and would immediately presume me as a suspect. Instead, I sat for an hour or so on a carpet crafted of sheep's wool and meticulously planned on how I would avenge my fallen without putting my neck on the line.

"I watched him lie there motionlessly as I contemplated on all the grief he had caused me while fighting the urge to personally slit his throat with every fibre of my being. The grand idea of sabotage came to me unassumingly as coincidence… He gave the order to massacre my people but his soldiers carried them out. They all had some karma coming in my books. Therefore, my logic was that by corrupting his mind, his soldiers would have their foremost war strategist incapable to lead them to a swift victory and most likely to a quick death for his luck of sound reasoning… Hannibal's vast and highly capable fleet had made incredible advancements covering great grounds towards Europe, the only obstacles between them and the destruction of Rome, being a legion of roman soldiers of whom they outnumbered ten to one and the treacherous alps that were steep and covered in thirty inches of snow.

"While pacing around searching for inspiration to devise a plan, I happened to come about the general's strategy table. From what I could gather, he had anticipated that going over the alps would have been the shortest route to the steps of Rome. However, the harsh elements would have cut down his fleet by over two by three and the weary survivors of the march downhill would be received by a roman legion armed to the teeth, awaiting their arrival, a certain massacre.

"'You shall set me free in front of an audience to witness that you no longer have a claim to me banishing and forgetting about me once I'm gone… You shall then march with all your soldiers towards Rome but you must go over the alps and fight to the bitter end.' I gave him his orders, of which he would be hell bent on fulfilling. *'Tu dismissed,'* the words to say to snap him out of his daze came to me like an instinct. He awoke from his euphoria confused but with the look of purpose in his face like he had something urgent to attend to at first light, as if a prosecutor on the morning's court date. He turned to face me then, broke eye-contact probably because he appeared to have no recollection of the chain of events that took place, and the last thing on his mind was how he was going to sexually assault me. By the tossed bedsheets and my ripped nightgown, he assumed he succeeded at the task, making the sight of me to him a guilt catalyst… By noon on that day, he would set me free, denouncing his claim of me in a small court where he soon after announced that the entire fleet would be marching for Rome by going over the alps as opposed to manoeuvring around it… Despite the certain death and depletion of ranks, this decision would cause. No one dared to defy their beloved leader and war hero, the great General Hannibal

Barca of Carthage, the first victim of my *omen omnibus* curse, a name I gave to it when I realised it worked on all men with lust in their heart… In other words, all men!… If you know your history, well, Father, you would know that Carthage was defeated because of their decision to hike the alps over going around it. My vengeance was the butterfly effect that led to the fall of Carthage! I made my way to the closest human encampment and to the next until I eventually ended up at the heart of civilization, Rome.

"There have been countless sins after that. I have honed the *omen omnibus* and can now distinguish between victim and lover. I have seen kingdoms rise and fall. I have lived through world wars, even started some just for kicks. Ironically as the years progressed and I lived beyond any human's natural lifespan without ageing, I lost a certain lust for life as a result of the promise of forever. It wasn't until I was awoken from deep slumber by an urge to start an architectural company in the late fifties that I got back my raison d'être.

"Knowing that my youth over time would not go unnoticed, I started it as a proxy company and remained a silent partner as it grew to unimaginable heights, and on my free time, I gathered skillsets and expertise. I studied architecture and engineering, medicine in private, and later reclaimed my company as a fifty-one-percent shareholder. The other thirty percent was in bonds. Rumour has it that they belonged to an anonymous silent partner that started the company in the fifties but liquidated and rebranded, giving her shares to the young CEO of the First Fruit Corporation and whose chair at boardrooms was always empty until the day she would decide to show up and formally introduce herself... Long story short, I was both fifty-one-percent shareholder and the other thirty percent was anonymously mine sixty years ago. The sole purpose was to change Clarence City's skyline when the time and the technological advancements had reached a minimum requirement to bring my vision to reality... You seem off and quiet. I hope you are not questioning my sanity," she asked Dionysus, eager to hear his feedback and prepared to go to great lengths to convince him.

He clenched his prayer beads that he was holding in his hands, asking for divine guidance in his mind on how to approach the mysterious woman's unlikely story without offending her, for she was highly delusional and probably secretly suffered from mental illness. That or she was yanking his chain. 'It would serve no good if I confronted her fantasies. I, therefore, must address her story as she believes it,' he thought to himself.

"You were right. This is a confession I shan't soon forget." They both laughed at his witty remark. "If your narrative is anything to go by, you have been alive for two and a half millennia as a result of selling your soul to a dark entity. You received immortality and a curse that gave you a supernatural sway over men that lust for you, a curse you deemed as the *omen omnibus* which, if my Latin isn't rusty enough, loosely translates to 'all men.' You were more or less responsible for the fall of Carthage and many others over time and are now living in the public eye with ambitions to rebuild the city to your own liking. I wonder out of all the sins a person in your unique circumstances would have accumulated, why you selected the one of your dark origin as one to be absolved? One might say that it's the sin that would scratch at the soul you claim you no longer have. The provable turn on the trail the ripple effect that led you to this very confession booth confessing your unfathomable story to an unassuming priest."

"I suppose so," she responded but could note the doubt and luck of conviction in his assessment of her confession.

"I also can't help but wonder why you chose me as the priest to confess too. There must be a reason beyond the fact that I am sworn by oath and to God to keep your secrets, for psychiatrists have doctor-patient confidentiality and are more inclined to listen to what you believe as truth regardless of how delusional it may come off as…"

"I did not come here seeking help, though. I feel like that is where you are drifting too, as the lord is my witness before leaving this booth. I will have you understand my crucible and how lucky you should consider yourself to hear my story." He noticed her tone had changed from a soft and playful-esque to an ominous threat responsive type and figured it was wise to attempt to de-escalate the situation.

"I don't mean to offend you but you have to see my predicament. Despite being fully concealed, I can see as clear as daylight that you truly believe in your narrative that you are a twenty-five-hundred-year-old sentient being and I would not be doing my duty as foremost a responsible adult than a priest if I did not recommend you to seek professional help." She could get where he was coming from and realised that for such a man with his wits and intelligence about him, he couldn't in good faith reconcile her frankly hard-to-believe story and feed her presumed delusions. She decided to change her technique to a more show-than-tell approach to put a close to any doubts.

"Dionysus, open the partition," she requested and he was just itching to slide it open, though it would have been a breach of Catholic ethics if he did.

"I'm afraid I cannot, as that would be a breach of trust for a priest to put a sin to a face," he responded as procedure but secretly hoped she wouldn't take no for an answer and insist.

"What if I give my consent? Would that suffice?"

"I suppose," he responded, now almost certain it was Genevieve in the booth. 'Trust her to find a loophole in a two-thousand-year-old Catholic tradition.'

"I feel like I should be making eye-contact, for I just confessed my darkest secret to you, a faceless friendly voice behind a wooden box. It feels distant and off. Consider my consent given." He pried the partition open to find a lady in a red dress seated with her legs folded. He took in her image from her red bottom black heels to the iconic infinity symbol on her right ankle and flirted his eyes up her long legs that ran down her curves like a majestic waterfall, her waistline as tight as a constrictor knot, her bosoms perky and evened out, and her hair as dark as a raven's feather up to her eyes that added to her facial symmetry.

"So when did you figure out it was me?" she asked, unsure whether he knew all along. It had been ages since she was unsure of anything. Uncertainty was refreshing and Dionysus was bringing thrills to her table she thought she would never get again. *What an interesting acquaintance he turned out to be!*

'What a vision she was!' he thought to himself before he answered, "I had my suspicions." They both chuckled and smiled at each other, almost as if complimenting each other for their shared appreciation of charismatic responses.

"Now that you know my story and can reconcile my narrative to my face, do you still have the same assessment that I should seek professional help?" she asked, setting back the original tempo at the risk of the offbeat turn of events of her exposing her visage to Dionysus would take away the building progression of her adagio by adding the excitement of seeing a familiar face as a potential adlib and possible route of deviation from topic.

"I'm afraid that now that I know it's you, I'm going to insist even more that you see someone about your case, as I wouldn't want anything bad to happen to you. It could be something as minor as a chemical imbalance." She was sure more than ever that he was not going to be convinced without a visual aid to case and point.

"Look into my eyes." It came off as a command more than a suggestion and he followed her instructions. She leaned forward and pushed her hair back, exposing her brown eyes to whatever light was available. He could feel blood rushing down his member as she licked her glossy lips that matched the colour of her dress and the bottom of her heels. "Pay attention." She was flattered his eyes had wandered off but needed him to remain objective.

"What are we supposed to accomplish here?" he asked.

"Just humour me. What colour are my eyes?"

"Perfect," he answered and she blushed.

"Focus!" She raised her tone to reset the mood.

"They are a deep brown."

"Great. Keep looking." He noticed a subtle colour change of her pupils from brown into the darkest shade of black he had ever seen, even more vexed as they slowly stretched vertically and the white in her eyes turned to a terrifying yellow. "What colour are my eyes now?" Her sweet voice had turned into a soul-piercing distorted sound that interestingly enough was horrifically audible!

He dropped his prayer beads that he was clenching in his hand as he gasped for air and it dawned on him that she was indeed who she said she was. "It's all true," he whispered while trying to catch his breath, hyperventilating. She went to his aid, her eyes and voice back to normal.

"Breathe! Breathe!" she repeated soothingly as she rubbed his back, nursing his panic attack till he was out of shock. "I know it's a lot to take in, so I shall give you time to process. For the next few weeks, I shall spend my evenings at the bar sitting at the bar counter where we first met. I'll be alone wearing a different tight and colourful dress every day and drinking Corpse Revivers back to back. I hope you shall join me at least once after you deeply think about whether you want to be part of my journey," she said right before she exited the confession booth, her hips swaying, and he watched in disbelief that she had shaken him to the core in less than an hour. One could only imagine what she could do to a man in a lifetime. There was no going back. The truth was out; the devil immortality and curses were all real and he began to doubt his path, faith, and existence.

He knew to turn to the only person he trusted and confided in, so he left to the veteran's cemetery, a bottle of Pappy Van Winkle Special Reserve in hand and walked over to Nathan's grave. He sat over the headstone that read: *Beloved friend and exceptional soldier,* poured two glasses of bourbon, and began to tell him of his encounter and eventually admitting his crisis in faith.

Chapter IX
Of Parlays and Compromise

He made his way through the dining area that would have passed as a king's banqueting table based on the spread laid out and the shiny silverware, crystal glasses, and pure cotton napkins on the tables placed with such precision.

'Who says crime doesn't pay?' he thought to himself as he walked towards the backyard where relatives and close friends to the Moretti family were gathered, guided by his concerned Sister Stefania, who on upon arrival gave him a warm embrace and welcome, for they had not seen each other in a while, her cause for concern being that the last time she saw John nearly half a decade ago, he was disowned and banished by Don Giani after he refused to be involved in their criminal income-generating activities. The room went silent and then flooded with whispers as he walked past the women and children heading to the table under the open-air atrium where the dons were seated smoking cigars and drinking grappa. He could make out some of the whispers. "That's Uncle John from the pictures." Some of the younger children of whom he had never met talked among themselves. "Why is he back now after so many years? Do you think he is a snitch sent by the authorities to break up our family?" He could overhear some of the conversations the women were having, with no regards to subtlety. He was soon standing in front of the don and his league of terrible men disguised as middle-aged dads in a family reunion gathering.

"The prodigal son returns." He blew out a puff from his cigar and reached out to hug him the rest of the family, cheering in joy of a reunion but mostly from relief that the don embraced him, as his reaction would have gone either way. "Welcome back, *mio figlio*. You look good," he whispered in his ear as they were locked in an embrace. "Time to eat."

"Manja! Manja! Manja!" they all rushed and walked with a sense of purpose, heading for the massive dining table. They had built up an appetite as one would expect seeing that their tradition entailed an empty stomach, a late lunch that would suffice as an early dinner, swiftly followed by wine, digestives espresso, and cigars throughout the night. They followed the masses a few paces behind, giving them some more time to go at their cigars before arriving at the dining table where the don enforced a no-smoking policy. Giani made a few inquiries into John's personal life on how he had been keeping, his marital status, and what he did for a living as they made their way to the dining area. To an untrained ear, it would sound like genuine concern but on the contrary, he was trying to deduce the kind of man John had become since he last saw him and why he came to the family function. If he said he was well and had never been better with great conviction, Don Giani would perceive that John still held his moral compass and holier-than-thee complex steady. If he was a married man with or without

sired children, the don could use them as leverage by threatening them to coerce John's actions as a future deterrent, and if he had a well-paying job, then money would not inspire, motivate, or corrupt him. The don was truly a man of great intellect, a calculative agent of pure malice. John knew he was dealing with a worthy adversary and did not dare drop his guard, for beyond their charming smiles and good bedside manner, the men in his immediate company were responsible for some truly atrocious crimes and a terrifying citywide chain of murders over nearly three decades.

They sat at the table, John close to the don so they could continue their subtle battle of wits. He had a quick look around and he thought if a flaming asteroid fell and hit the dining area of the estate. It would have in one swipe gotten rid of ninety percent of the crime rate in the city, for the heads of all four Italian families under Don Giani were present at the table.

On the far left sat Don Salvatore of the Salvatore crime family that focused on racketeering and blackmail social issues and propaganda, think mob public relations. Then there was Don Castillo of the Castillo mob. Theirs was an even darker specialty. They dealt in human trafficking in form of prostitution, the oldest profession in the world, getting girls from Eastern Europe, South America, and Southeast Asia, sourcing them from other global crime factions and having them delivered to Clarence City where they would be managed by the Castillo mob henchmen that used human-violating methods like heroin as wages and a backhand strike as the go-to disciplinary action should they fail to raise the quota.

Then came Don Figiani of the Figiani crime family. They handled drugs supplying in all sections of the city. Then finally came Don Mingetti of the Mingetti crime family that dealt in guns and illegal firearms. They armed all branches under the Moretti family with some untraceable pistols, rifles, and heavy artillery, and they also armed the other inferior gangs for a profit.

They soon consumed their dinner and the don excused himself and his comrades to go to talk business in the privacy of his study. "Mio Figlio, join us." He followed the made-men as they walked through the study doors and locked it behind him. Giani had taken the initiative of arriving first and had taken a seat on his iconic boss's chair while he smoked a cigar. He looked into John's eyes, speaking without speaking, and his smile faded to an aggressive grin, letting John know that his hospitality was over and he had to explain his reason for visiting the estate.

"Why are you here?" he asked as Don Salvatore unbuttoned his gun holster, proving what he suspected.

"I'm sure you know how I feel about the family business. It's not a well-kept secret that I don't approve of benefiting from other people's pain and suffering."

"Save it for the pope," Salvatore answered. The rest chuckled, all but John. "I find myself at your doorstep after swearing to never return, leaving me as subject to the old quote of necessity leading to strange bed fellows."

He puffed out his cigar. "It must be something serious for you to ask for my help. I'm the last person you would turn to," Giani mentioned as he rivalled at the sight of John's humble pie feast. "Ironically, you are both my problem and only solution. As mentioned, I'm a junior partner in a development company known as the First Fruit Corporation. You might be familiar with it. They got a contract to rebuild the city skyline from our late mayor. I'm here as a courtesy to inform you that we shall be venturing in your turf, putting up buildings in places you might not want buildings put up by government mandate. I know your influence runs deep and you would be better off a friend than enemy. I'm here to ask for your support and blessing, as this could be mutually beneficial in the grand scheme of things."

"Well, thank you for the courtesy visit and information., I heard that the mayor gave some lady and her company the equivalent of the key to the city without my consent... She must be very captivating because right before he died, he raged about her beauty and her charm. I'm willing to play ball, but first you have to kiss the ring come back into the warm embrace of the family, learn from the best, and when the time is right, assume your rightful position as Don." John flirted with the notion that he would find a way to evade such a horrible fate and that it would be a long time before he would be required to take Don's seat, so he thought. He ran a priority assessment in his mind, given that his needs to get the corporation of the mob to begin their building projects was more immediate than the consequences of joining the family business. He leaned forward and kissed Don Giani's ring, symbolising an acceptance of terms and pledging of loyalty, a decision he would come to regret in hind sight.

"You can proceed with your projects. I shall put the word out that you are under our protection and I'll give you some time to come up with an offering for the family. Keep in mind we will be sacrificing a lot of revenue-generating operations to accommodate you and the First Fruit Corporation, so make it generous and worth our while or else…"

"I appreciate the help, Don," John answered, disrupting him before he could finish stating the consequences, proving to the don that he saw the full spectrum and knew what he was getting himself into. He gave him a hug and whispered, "It's good to have you back," as John left for the driveway in disbelief how easy getting in bed with the devil was. Traditionally, it was getting out that proved to be challenging.

He needed a drink and the caress of a woman. He pulled out his phone and began searching for the number of a girl he had gone out for dinner with a few nights before they matched in an online dating app. He was intent on having her over to his townhouse to share a bottle of wine and hopefully she would spend the night tussling under his sheets, scratching his back and moaning in pleasure. He snapped out of his daydream and began taking the much-needed action to make it a reality. He selected the contact Jacklyn Serabona and sent her a text that read: *"Evening I have been thinking about you more than I should be and now more than ever. I'm heading home to open up a twenty-year-old chateau Margo from a special cabinet in my cellar. However, I have always gathered that a bottle of wine is only as good as the company it's shared with rather than grape variety or vintage. If you would care to join me tonight, it would be the best bottle of wine I've had yet."*

She soon responded, *"Send me the location. Fair warning. I might be overdressed currently at the journalist awards. It's a black-tie event. The dress I'm wearing might give you a heart attack."*

He instructed the driver to drive quicker. He had the urgent business of romance to attend to.

The door flung open and he rushed into his bedroom where he hurriedly removed his suit that reeked of cigar smoke. He took a shower to wash off a day's work odour and slipped into a casual outfit, a silk burgundy shirt, some black corduroy pants, and Tom Ford slip-on loafers he had bought a week ago, dabbing some Tuscan-leather cologne on his wrist and neck to complete his outfit. He planned on keeping the ambiance as homely and intimate as possible to give her the impression of himself in his natural element. He then proceeded by lighting some scented candles in the living room and grabbing two of his costly crystal Bordeaux glasses, preparing a cheese platter with red and white grapes, crackers, jams as condiments, and five selections of cheese, making his way to the cellar where he grabbed the chateau morgue bottle from the top rack, dusting the ten-thousand-dollar bottle and prepping a decanter to pour it in to let it react with fresh air. Working in their family restaurant in his teens made him well versed in wine knowledge and all things food and beverage.

He put his romancing paraphernalia for the evening on a glass coffee table and sat on a sofa directly behind it, waiting patiently for his guest of honour to arrive while playing scenarios in his head on what he would say to her to get her out of that tight dress she claimed she would come clad in.

Shortly after, his doorbell rang and he sprang into action, opening the door and ready to receive her. He gasped at the sight of how ravishing she looked in a black dress that hugged her tight like lovers reunited, drawing a map of her physique provocatively exposing but at the same harmony leaving just the right amount to the imagination. "You were right. My heart just skipped a beat or two," he complimented her.

"Thank you." She blushed as he let her in and took her coat, guiding her to the sofa.

She was flattered when she saw the spread he had set out for her in such a short time. His efforts to please her did not go unnoticed. He grabbed a wine opener and skilfully opened the bottle of wine as she nibbled on the cheese platter in front of her. "Wow! You know your way around a wine bottle."

"Thanks. I worked in a family-owned restaurant as a teenager... Picked up a few things." She smiled and took comfort that the man who was entertaining her knew more beyond the mediocre perimeters of privilege.

"There is more to you than meets the eye," she responded, fully aware that if she let the conversation drift to an exchange of compliments, they would be at it for quite some time.

"... And I intend to bear all. I hope you feel the same." She was impressed by how he turned what most would consider an open-ended question into one for her that required a variety of answers to give beyond a measly yes, no, or thanks. He took a sniff of the cork of the wine to detect if there were any abnormal aromas like strong acidity or mould as wines of such vintage where delicate and could get ruined easily if not properly stored. He then proceeded to pour down to the last drop of the precious elixir into a decanter made of crystal, swirling it and placing it on the table, giving it time to breathe a term that wine connoisseurs use that means to let the wine react with oxygen. He could have very easily have done all the wine preparation before she arrived but he wanted to show her his prowess.

She had a quick glance around the room and came to the conclusion that he lived a comfortable life, financially at least, based on the ten-thousand-dollar bottle and expensive artwork on walls. The crystal chandelier on the ceiling and Italian marble on the floors had her convinced that he didn't struggle financially like most people in the city did.

"Nice place. The First Fruit Corporation must really take care of its model employees…"

"… Well, in the spirit of baring all, this is not a result of what I do for a living." He sat relatively close to her and leaned back on the sofa.

"You're from a well-off family?" she asked, her curiosity fully peaked.

"One that I want very little to do with but have no choice but to maintain a relationship with."

"Sounds complicated." She appreciated that he was opening up to her and she was learning about him. "I intend to get deeply involved with you, all in good time so I might as well tell you the darker side of my story now so you could run for the hills as opposed to you finding out much later."

He leaned forward and poured her a glass of the ruby-red elixir and soon poured one for himself. "The family I want nothing to do with is the Moretti family. My uncle is Don Giani Moretti. My father was Don Francesco Moretti." She briefly chocked on a sip of wine that was in her mouth and then swallowed it with a gasp of air. "Before you judge me too soon, no one can control what family they are born into, and as soon as I figured out that my family profits off the misery of others I disowned and cut off all ties for almost half a decade. It wasn't till today that I had to go bargain safety for our men working on building the new FFC buildings in mob turf the whole necessity leading to strange bed fellows of it all."

"I understand your predicament but understand mine. Your family has caused a lot of pain and misery in the city. I can't look past the fact that you are mob royalty and might one day assume the title of Don. I can, however, see that you are a good, compassionate man and I intend on being there to keep you that way but as a friend," she defined her boundaries and spoke with reason but her heart felt true desire and yearning for John and her eyes gave her away. "Friends who occasionally make love," she added, softening the blow and revealing a light at the end of the tunnel for John, giving him the incline that if he remained a good honourable man, he would eventually win her over.

It had been a day full of negotiations and compromise, first with the don and now with Jessica, with an ideal bargain to become lovers and a settled compromise to become friends that have sex casually. He needed a win and enjoyed the idea of the latter. He leaned over to kiss her and she kissed him back. They finished the wine and he achieved his evening's ambitions of drink and pleasurable activities under his silk sheets with her till dawn, a sweet end to a day full of parleys and compromises.

Chapter X
Paralysie De Choix
'Choice Paralysis'

Three days had passed since she came into his confession booth and shook him to his core. Since then, he couldn't bring himself to go to the bar counter to meet her, as he was going through personality and character-redefining phases that entailed self-doubt, denial, and a complete loss of faith. He, however, kept face and continued his duties as a priest, masking his exponential crisis and compensating for it with a facade of even stronger conviction in his beliefs to his congregation.

He was sober for the first time in a long time. He needed to keep his wits about him, a clear mind to process what Genevieve had showed and told him, questioning all he had been taught and conditioned to believe by society, religion, and modern-day science.

"Her existence should not be possible," he reasoned but then again, he saw with his own two eyes of twenty-twenty vision how horrendous her serpent-like eyes turned, and heard with his own ears her sweet voice change to the state of abomination.

'A parlour trick, an elaborate prank from a bored eccentric woman with too much time on her hands.' He tried to rationalise what he had witnessed but he knew in his heart of hearts that it wasn't the case. Hers was a tale that was unlikely, improbable, and impossible but yet the bitter facts stung his intellectual pallet. He would tear down the entire encounter down to its last hypothetical fabric just like the highly trained soldier he once was. There were no devices on her to simulate her terrifying distorted voice. She couldn't have been wearing automated contact lenses, for her eyes were the same colour they were when they first met at the bar, a deep sexy brown until they were not.

He began to drift towards the likelihood of her story, as all the vigorous checkboxes he had set out to prove otherwise were checked out. The more he got convinced of her tale, a crucial piece from the house of cards that was his fragile mind state came undone, priming it for a complete tumble when he was fully convinced, of which he soon was.

He had finished his afternoon mass and was heading towards the library to catch up on history, for if Genevieve was truly an immortal being that had lived for over two and a half millennia, there would most likely be some record pictures or stories of her over time. Her tale was seared in his mind and he remembered where she said it all began in a small fishing village somewhere between modern-day Iraq and Iran, between four intersecting rivers and a sea that was forming, slowly engulfing an island, leaving only a tree at its peak, giving off an optic illusion of a floating tree when viewed from the shore. That's where he would begin his research.

As a priest, he was well versed in his Bible stories. Based on what she told him of a tree and a serpent, he immediately thought of the story of creation, the story of Adam, Eve, the tree of the forbidden fruit, and the serpent. He couldn't help but shake the feeling that her story was somehow derivative of the creation theory. He was soon at the library and went directly to the historical geography section with urgency, peeked curiosity, and an insatiable need to know.

He found what he was looking for an atlas of what the ancient map of the world would have looked like and another of what it looked like currently. He opened up the page of contents for reference and searched for keywords like Iraq and Iran, which was the former Persian Empire, impatiently flipping through the pages for he had a hunch and wouldn't let up till he found some answers and there it was! Four rivers that would have intersected somewhere in the Persian Empire just like she said! He searched for an explanation on his modern-day atlas and he found that two of the rivers and point of intersection had been submerged by a forming water body that would eventually become the Gulf Sea. It made sense, since from his experience as a soldier in the region, he knew that the Gulf Sea was only five hundred meters deep. He hurriedly ran to the religion section grabbing a Bible and frantically flipped through the chapter of genesis. He got goose bumps as his working theory started to unfold.

He knew right where to look. In Genesis chapter two, verse nine to fourteen, he ran his finger on the words as he read aloud. He didn't want to miss a thing. "Now a river flowed out of Eden to water the garden, and from there it divided and became four rivers. The name of the first is Pishon. It flows around the whole land of Havilah, where there is gold. The name of the second river is Gihon. It flows around the whole land of Cush. The name of the third river is Tigris. It flows east of Assyria. And the fourth river is the Euphrates."

He gasped in shock and got lightheaded as his theory was fully confirmed that the submerging island from Genevieve's confession with the tree at its peak was actually the garden of Eden and the tree now somewhere deep in the Gulf Sea was the tree of life. The hairs on the back of his neck rose when he thought of the serpent, the same serpent that tempted Eve, the original sinner and the dark entity from her vision or spirit astro projection as she called. It was none other than the deceiver of men! "The devil! Lucifer, star of the morning!" He found the nearest seat as his wobbly feet would soon be unable to support his weight, a result from the shock of his discovery.

As soon as he caught his breath, he mastered the courage to continue his research. He gathered some books on the second Punic War to gather information about General Hannibal Barca and his war path to Rome. He found out that just as Genevieve said he was recruiting villagers to join his ranks on the march to Rome and he would burn the villages and massacre the occupants, of those who refused to join his cause, leaving only the most beautiful young women to be his concubines and gifts to reward his high-ranking soldiers that were exceptional in battle. He also noted that his empire fell because of an ill-advised decision he took to climb over the alps as opposed to manoeuvring around it, a decision that came as a surprise to his army and came at the high cost of depletion of his ranks and eventually the fall of Carthage. He was considered the greatest strategists' general to have lived even to modern-day standards and allegedly met his demise by committing 'suicide' in poetic fashion in 183 BC after being exiled to Bithynia, a region in Northern Turkey after the second Punic War. The Romans, seeking to bring Hannibal to justice, demanded the Bithynian king to hand him over. 'No doubt the effect of her *omen omnibus*,' he thought.

He put away his research and headed to the veterans' graveyard. He needed counsel with the one person who he truly confided in and wouldn't judge even if he could. He walked over to the headstone and began to converse with the memory of Nathan.

"Didn't bring you any bourbon today? I find myself in need of your listening ear again for the second time this week. Don't be concerned the world is not ablaze… yet." he chuckled at his own humour. Nathan always appreciated his witty banter. "I just found out that the devil is real and if balance is anything to go by his extreme opposite, God must be too.

"The woman I told you about, I have no doubt she is who she says she is. The things she must have seen over time the forming of the church, the reign of Cesar, the fall of Rome, and even maybe the Crucifixion of Jesus. Imagine how exciting yet terrifying being in her presence after knowing her truth can be? It's no wonder she is in the public eye and yet remains the epitome of anonymity. If the world were to know the truth about her, there would be pandemonium, panic, and a worldwide crisis in religion on all platforms in a day and age of modern-day deities. People would start praying to her.

"I realised that God brought her to my life for a purpose, for she walks unprotected in such dangerous times in Clarence City that the line between good and evil fades over time and she has been alive for over two millennia. Therefore, hers must be nearly non-existent. That if she can live forever and do good for humanity with the limitless resources, she has and is well on her way to acquire more. She could be mankind's salvation, but if she is corrupted and goes about eternity wreaking havoc like a goddess of destruction, then she could be mankind's doom… This is precisely why I must break the vows I took in honour of your memory, to do no harm to others but to guide lost souls and the misguided to the light of the best versions of themselves. I thought I could best do that as a priest but with recent developments, I can't in good faith continue life as before, knowing of her existence. I shall leave the church and protect and guide her with an iron fist and occasionally if someone is unwise enough to make an attempt on her life or wellbeing. They shall face the business end of my firearm.

"Goodbye, my friend. I'm afraid I shall not be able to show up as frequently as I used to. There is a lot of character redefining and work to be done. She awaits at the bar based on what she told me and I'm four days late from our initial appointment and therefore I must find her right away. Rest well, my friend." He touched the headstone and walked away on course to the arch bishop's residence. He went to him to officially discuss his terms on exiting the church.

Genevieve took pride in the fact that she could read people like literary agents read books but nothing in this life is certain and a small margin of error could turn to a full-blown disaster. She took comfort in the fact that Dionysus did not show up at the bar for the last three days, for had he shown up at the rendezvous on the first night of her proposition , it would likely be that he would have come to say goodbye and part ways with her but the fact that half the week had passed since her offer, it gave her the perception that he was conflicted and weighing his options or had a case of choice paralysis, indecisiveness brought on by too many options on his next course of action. She wasn't expecting him till the proverbial equivalent of 'last call for check-in' at the airport. That would be sometime between the fifth day till the seventh from the seven-day deadline she had given him while exiting the confession booth.

She wasn't expecting him. Yet, she showed up to the bar religiously in a devilish dress. Her drink was running out but she was pacing herself as she had too many over the week and the taste was becoming monotonous when she heard a familiar voice behind her ask the bartender at the counter for a bourbon neat and a corpse reviver. She turned to find Dionysus behind her in a Tom Ford three-piece suit that brought his Greek-god physique to light far better than the priest's attire did. "Took you long enough," she said as they both chuckled and he pulled up a chair at the counter next to her.

They had a few drinks and the bar counter started to get crowded. They both understood that they were long overdue for a conversation of pressing matters as opposed to the small talk they were currently engaging in to break the ice, the crowded bar counter serving as a perfect excuse to find some privacy to converse. "Shall we move to the private dining area?" he asked and she nodded, approving his idea with a look of relief on her face that he finally caught on the conditions of his environment.

Chapter XI
A Vow of Servitude

The private dining area also served as a wine cellar. They walked through the unoccupied room as she looked around appreciating the architectural designs of the wing of her favourite bar and restaurant that she had never been in. Their server was soon behind them with their partially consumed drinks on a tray as they had moved from bar counter to private dining area.

She didn't know it yet but she was sitting at the same table Don Giani and Paul, the late mayor, had their last encounter, of which he was poisoned as a consequence of making ill-advised decisions that went against the best interests of the mob due to Genevieve's *omen omnibus*. The don was a creature of habit and he had grown particularly fond of the table she and Dionysus had occupied. One who could see the full spectrum like an author reading his scripted plot coming along would argue that the table was the equivalent of Hitler's red telephone that he used to give orders of genocide to be carried out, for on that table, he sanctioned assassinations even carried some out as well whenever he dabbled in his illegal firearms and human trafficking apparatus and all the terrible things being the don of the Moretti family entailed. He preferred to do them while seated on that particular table that typically would have been reserved for him alone had he not been out of town. "Bring another round after fifteen minutes or so," he gave the server instructions and he could immediately perceive that they were not to be disturbed. *"Capito singore,"* he responded as the habitual response he would give to the usual occupant of the table who was heavily associated with his preference of service in Italian. "I mean understood, sir." They chuckled as he made a quick exit, embarrassed.

"You shook me to my core. Do you know that?" It was a rhetorical question, for she obviously did. "To the extent that I just gave up my priesthood and denounced any oath I previously might have taken."

She wasn't as surprised as one might have assumed she would be at hearing how hard to process her story was, the changes and difficulties the person she confessed to went through. She was, however, impressed at how quickly Dionysus adapted compared to the people she had previously come clean to in the past. Even Cleopatra went mad and clutched a venomous snake with no known anti-venoms upon finding out who she truly was. Yet, here he was calm, composed, and surprisingly collected.

"Your existence proves how historical and modern-day beliefs on religion and science are baseless speculations. I shall be entirely grateful that you trusted me with your incredible eye-opening story that has set me on a new path of self-discovery, not to mention my sense of purpose fully engaged and stimulated.

"If you would have me, I would like to walk with you hand-in-hand till the end of my days, listening to your experiences over the past, documenting the actual occurrences of history according to your witness and in exchange. I'll take a vow of servitude to you to use my unique training as a soldier and skillset as a bringer of death to protect you, my gathered experience as a priest to guide you as your true north to becoming a practitioner of moral human ethics. For I believe God put you in my path for a reason and with your potential and my guidance you could be an eternal force of good and mankind's salvation in turn earning your redemption and if my suspicions are correct, regaining all that was taken from you."

His intuition filled her with awe, as typically whoever she told her story to either ran for hills or saw her as a goddess among men, bowing to her every will, throwing flowers at her feet, and smothering her with unwanted attention, not him though. He was different. He truly saw her and could somehow piece together her confliction and apathy in pleasures of life that the average human-being revelled in, like starting a family and going on vacation.

"I will not learn to love you just to lose you to mortality. Our relationship needs to be one of objective purpose for the greater good of mankind." She brought up her terms and he soon added the convincing blow that would sway her to accept his vow.

"Agree to these terms and you shall have me as a comrade for as long as I live, and should I have sons, they too shall embark on the same journey." Her heart pounded out of her chest for a man with his good days almost behind him. He managed to promise companionship for eternity to the best of his ability.

"I accept your vow and shall honour you as much you do me." They smiled at each other, her pearly whites partially exposed , she licked her lower lip and gently bit on it as it slowly slipped back to its normal resting position. He felt a rush down his spine as he imagined them wrapped around his member, attempting to siphon out his whole being.

"Beg your pardon, the drinks you requested for." The server was back fifteen minutes to the dot and right on time to deliver what would be their celebratory drink of their new partnership. They finished their previous round as they were both fond of alcohol and did not believe in wasting a drop of it. The server collected their empty glasses and left the table, leaving behind the fresh serving of drinks he had come with as he hastily left, giving them privacy.

"To eternity and a partnership full of wonders and accomplishments." They raised their glasses and clinked them before taking a sip and putting them down as they stared at each other, priming themselves for the next phase of their conversation now that they had addressed the most pressing of matters. Conversation was leading towards ad lib and organic thoughts as opposed to scripted and well thought of.

Chapter XII
La Petite Mort
'The Small Death'

"The dress you wore tonight really compliments your physique." It had been the first verbal compliment he had given her ,now that he was free from the restrictions of being a priest, he could indulge beyond the lusty looks and wondering eyes that would flirt down from her dome to her feet.

"You look and talk quite different from the priest I met in the bar... It's sexy," she added to distract him from lingering on the sudden changes he had made in his life, getting him on the same page and encouraging the sexual tension to build to what she hoped would be a night of passion.

He looked at her brown sexy eyes, her dark hair running down to her well-oiled shoulder blades and the tips of her perky bosoms printed out on her dress. She wasn't wearing a bra. She knew what was on his mind, for it was on hers too, and were they not in public, she would sit on his face and rock back and forth vigorously till she exploded in body-seizing nectar-dripping pleasure. He was a bit out of practice and hadn't caught on the full potential the night brought with it. She kicked of her pumps and started running her feet down his leg for a good measure. They sipped their drinks in silence but spoke volumes in body language. Although he tried to appear unbothered while she ran her foot up his crotch area, his noticeable bulge proved otherwise.

Showing finesse while working her foot over his pants and getting a feel of his hard protruding member that seemed to be about to tear the stitches at the seams of his pants. Her eyes widened in erotic surprise of how well-endowed he was. He measured over her entire foot from heel to toe and she was a Size Eight 'US.' She slipped her shoes on and put a halt on her mischievous activities when she spotted the server approaching their table for a quality check.

"I hope everything is to your liking?"

"… More than you can imagine," she responded and he smiled, unaware that she wasn't referring to the service but rather how her evening was turning out. "We will have the check now, please." The server brought the bill back and placed it in front of Dionysus. She quickly grabbed it but he protested, insisting that he should be the one to settle it. She typically wouldn't allow it but she realized that it had been a while since he entertained a woman in a restaurant romantically and he needed to pay for their consumption to remind him of the satisfaction of hosting a lady. They finished their drinks, grabbed their coats, his bulge visible but fading. They both had erotic thoughts in their head. She was soaked in nectar.

Her chauffeur was pulling through the pickup area. Dionysus stood beside her without verbal confirmation on whether he was to join her but there was an inexplicable certainty that they were leaving together.

Her town car pulled up the driveway. He opened the door for her and she entered, pulling his free arm as she moved a seat over, making room for him to join her, hence the unspoken consent he was waiting for and that he quickly picked up on as he hopped in and shut the door behind him. "Take me home."

"Certainly, Miss Henrietta." The chauffeur shut the automatic privacy partition that was blacked out by paint and sealed with rubber, leaving it opaque and completely sound-proof. The tint on the windows was completely dark. Pedestrians and drivers couldn't make out what was happening in the car unless the door was open.

They could have easily made love in the car and none would have been the wiser but she wanted to savour him, as rushing a man who hadn't felt the warmth of a woman in many years could lead to a pleasurable minute and an uneventful evening. She knew just what to do as she started to kiss on his neck while running her hands on his chest, slowly working past his abdomen to his crotch area. His member throbbed and demanded release from the constrictions of his trousers. It was almost as if she was obliged to listen to it as she opened his zipper and adjusted his briefs, letting out the throbbing and edgy probe of his anatomy out of its restrictions. She gently stroked it, feeling its sharp edges and the veins on its ridges. She could barely fit her hand around it from its girth, working from base to tip in pure shock at his endowment.

She knew that for him to be a sufficient lover throughout the night, he would need a break after his first release and intended to use the most of the thirty-minute drive till she got to her place siphoning his being, removing the physical manifestation of his lack of practice from its wrinkly habitat. Hopefully that would be enough time for him to recover and be ready to properly use his tool when they arrived and had their first drink.

She looked in his eyes as she stroked up and down the abnormally long member and then made his heart stop for a few seconds when she leaned forward and put it in her mouth. His tender skin came into contact with her wet kisses. He could hear her gag and gasp as she slobbed and playfully twirled her tongue around conventionally unreachable parts of his probe that made him erupt like Mount Vesuvius…her mouth being Pompeii. She then swallowed his lava, vacuuming off any traces of it while firmly gripping the storage unit, squeezing out any creation fluid that might have survived her vicious suction, leaving him dry as the Sahara.

He sighed in pleasure, as he had never experienced such prowess. She finished off and his member started to lose its enthusiasm. She tucked it back in his pants, closed the zipper, leaned over, and kissed him. "It's my turn when we get to my place," she whispered in his ear. His knees were still wobbly from pleasure but he nodded in acceptance as she leaned on his chest, listening to his irregularly fast heartbeat slowing down as he recovered from the sorcery she had practised on him. "Wake me when we arrive," she seductively whispered as her sense of foresight told her that she wouldn't get much sleep that night.

Jacklyn was wrapping up another long tiresome day. It had been a week since her last encounter with John. Their night of passion was etched in her mind as she thought of it between bouts of productivity at work, making her moist and causing peculiar throbs before she would snap out of her daydreams and proceed with whatever task was at hand.

As much as she thought of him, she ignored his text messages and phone calls, for she could not get over the fact that he was pretty much the next heir to the Moretti crime family throne. She had set out conditions of their relationship, for she couldn't let herself get deeply involved with such a man. Despite him being honourable and having a moral compass unlike many of the men in his family, she figured his fate was sealed and he would eventually fall into the ways of his kin if the Biblical quote that says, "The sins of the father shall be visited upon the son," was anything to go by.

Yet, she craved for him like water to a stranded man in the desert. Her strategy was to compartmentalise their relationship to define it as a friendship of physical intimacy at odd hours of the night and out-of-town getaway escapades, for she did not want to be publicly identified as a known associate of him due to his family complications.

The conditions, however, were conducive to her terms. It was dark half, the city was asleep and the rest were out romancing or making love. "I deserve companionship just like them," she reasoned as she justified to her better judgment why she was reaching out to John as she pulled out her cell phone and poetically texted, *"I know it's late but I have been thinking about you all week now more than ever… Can you host?"*

John on the other end was about to turn in from another exhausting day when his phone beeped. He couldn't hide his excitement when he saw who the text was from and what it said. He had no intention of drinking that night until she asked him of his whereabouts and he casually responded, *"Yes, I'd love to have you over. My evening just got a whole lot better. Martinis?"*

She chuckled at how he was always ready to receive her. It warmed her heart. She got a taxi and set course to his townhouse.

She was soon at his doorstep where he had a vodka martini with olives in hand for her when he opened the door. She found his theatrics hilarious as they sat on the sofa they sat on when he poured his heart out to her and was ill-received by her to an extent.

He was traditional, not the kind of man to skip formalities, but they both knew why she was at his place at such an odd hour of the night. They finished their drinks and he kissed her, wrapping his arm under her knees and the other behind her back. He lifted her up and she giggled as he carried her to the bedroom.

He threw her on the bed that broke her fall. It bounced and wobbled as it absorbed her weight. His vision was majestic from the angle she was seeing him from, making her lust for him even more. She quickly kicked off her heels and raised her legs as he helped her take off her skirt.

She had no panties on and his member turned hard as a rock at the sight of her womanhood. He took off her blouse, her bosoms plump and perky, no doubt an effect he had on her. He stripped, exposing his complete nude as she already had, leaning forward and kissing her, his entire body weight on her. She kissed him back as he worked his way down her neck and under her earlobes while caressing her thighs, shoulders, and back. He worked his way down her right bosom, putting its hard peak in his mouth, twirling his tongue around it and playing with the other and then alternating until she gasped in stimulation and pushed his head lower, letting him know she was ready for the next part of his exploration.

He did as instructed, showering her with kisses on her stomach in a descending pattern until he was at his destination. She smelled of coconut and pineapples, which made sense to him, seeing how her favourite drink was a pina colada and she had consumed plenty over the week. She groaned at the touch of his tongue. Her lower thighs between his shoulders as she thrust and arched her back towards his face, his rough hands stretched out, caressing her bosoms as he teased with his tongue and pulled with his lips until she dug her nails into his forearms, letting him know that she was about to reach *le petite mort*. He quickly reset to a mount position, penetrated his member into her womanhood, and struck and thrust vigorously and repetitively as she let go, shaking and convulsing, spilling her nectar on his chest and pelvic region, leaving a puddle of love on where she lay. He held her tight and they fell asleep in each other's arms.

"I think we are here," Dionysus told Genevieve as he gently ran his hand on her shoulder to wake her. She stretched her arms and kissed him. The chauffeur had come to a complete stop and the doorman knocked on the car window, giving them sufficient warning that he was going to open the door. They exited the car and made their way to her penthouse. She pushed the last button of the elevator and they were slingshot to the last floor of the luxurious apartment buildings. She had the entire floor to herself. He tried not to look intimidated by her, for she was truly an impressive woman. They walked past her living room that had Persian rugs on the marble floors, white leather sofas that had the initials LV on the pillow cushions, and historical artifacts in glass safes on display, of which he assumed were her mementos, knowing who she was.

They finally got to her chambers, a massive bed covered in silk cream sheets, a huge television mounted on the wall, a sofa similar to the one in the living room, a bar counter full of a variety of alcoholic beverages, and cocktail paraphernalia. On the countertop were ingredients of her favourite cocktail. She leaned in for a kiss. "I'll go freshen up. Make us a drink, one part lime juice, one part gin, half a part orange liquor, a dash of absinthe shake and pour in the glass. Ingredients are at the countertop." She instructed before making her way to the bathroom as he attempted to prepare two corpse revivers.

He put all ingredients in the shaker, added some ice, gave it a nice shake to chill and dilute and then he served the drinks on some two crystal coupe glasses. She was soon out of her bathroom in a bathrobe and nothing else! He could feel his member slowly recovering from the drainage of its contents on the ride to her place. She could notice the glow of lust in his eyes slowly return but she would finish her drink over nonsexual banter until she could see his bulge as enthusiastic as it was in the car.

"Out of curiosity, who else did you tell your story to?" Dionysus asked, giving her the opportunity to deviate from sexual topic.

"I had just found my niche in Rome as a merchant of opium ,spice ,fragrances and wine, a position I of course assumed with aid from my *omen omnibus*. I noticed a repeat of clientele, servants sent to procure the items I sold frequently and in bulk. I inquired to whom they belonged to so as to thank them as loyal customers. Turns out they were under the employ of Marcus Antonius." He stared at her in complete marvel as she told him yet another incredible encounter. "You might know him as Mark Anthony. He was entertaining a lady who would turn out to be one of my best friends, Cleopatra. She was truly eccentric and I loved her for it.

"She once made a bet with him that she would have the most expensive dinner for two. Marcus arrived expecting a huge banquet only to find a simple mediocre spread at the table. He enjoyed what was put out for him and said that the dinner was basic and did not cost the fortune she had promised… She then had her servant procure the equivalent of a very strong white vinegar that I had in my inventory and used it to dissolve a massive pearl valued at approximately one hundred million dollars today's equivalent in her cup, drinking the concoction as a digestive, winning her the bet and making her dinner even by today's standards the most expensive meal ever consumed.

"As our friendship grew, I eventually confided in her and she got green with envy at the fact that I would live forever without ageing and she wouldn't. She decided to re-enact my origin story by getting the largest asp Egyptian cobra she could get and letting it bite her foot like the serpent did to me in hopes that the dark entity would come to her and grant her immortality. He did not and she passed away painfully. I then vowed to keep my truth hidden, that is until I met you."

While she told her story, her bosom slipped out of cover playfully. She could feel the gown slip and a cold breeze make its way in but she ignored it, almost as if she was doing it on purpose and it was working. His member was harder than it had been when her luscious lips and playful tongue were on it.

The bulge in his pants was back and she couldn't take her eyes off it. He noticed and put his drink down as he began to kiss her, warming his hands on her thighs before bringing them up to completely take off her gown…

She stood from the sofa and walked to the bed, strutting at complete nude, bending over, and moving on all fours like a feline. He watched seated, taking in the view of her from the , the soles of her feet, the curve of her womanhood, the bulk of her thighs and buttocks held together by her tight waist, flat belly, and perky milk globes that responded to his touch by getting hard at the tips. She turned and lay on her back, seductively raising her legs in the air as he hurriedly took his clothes off. "Do you have your collar?" she asked as he laughed, assuming she was joking but she wasn't. "Put it on," she commanded and he reached for his trousers on the floor and pulled out the tool of his former trade that he kept as a memento, a priest's collar that was about to be used in a manner the pope would not approve. He put it on and hopped onto the bed, making his way to her to kiss her lips but she put her index finger across his mouth, nudging him towards where she preferred her kisses.

The intoxicating smell of roses and lavender got stronger as he made his way down to her lady garden. He stuck his index finger in and pushed it towards the roof of her womanhood to a rough surface that he stimulated by making a come-here motion and put the entire top and most sensitive part of her womanhood in his mouth, his tongue making a wave motion as its tip did a vigorous flick upon contact , his finger and mouth working in rhythm to give her a synchronised inward and outward eruptions while she pinched and twisted her hard, sensitive chest raisins. He continued his work for some time and noticed that her back was arched and she begun to convulse, making him even more confident in his actions as he proceeded to feast on her with more enthusiasm until she was mad with pleasure.

His lips on her womanhood felt incredible and she wasn't about to have that feeling gone just yet in exchange for mediocre penetration. She did her iconic manoeuvre that left her in the mount position, dripping nectar from her first eruption on him, he had given her one but she was kin to orchestrate another for herself and just needed his mouth to complete her objective. She asked for consent to sit on his face. He lifted her, transferring her mount from his pelvic region to his facial area. She grabbed the headstand and started rocking back and forth on his tongue that he had stuck out. His hands made their way to her milk globes as he grabbed her bosoms and rubbed on their protruding tips with his thumbs as she rocked, swayed, and grinded. Friction from the tiny hairs that the wax strip missed while she groomed herself the previous night tickled his upper lip and oral region. She let out a loud moan and sat on him motionlessly with her eyes closed and legs trembling, nearly suffocating him. He knew not to let the golden opportunity pass as he quickly lifted her up and tossed her on her back, grabbing two pillows from her massive bed, piling them on top of each other, and placing them on her lower back, elevating her pelvic region.

He stuck his member in her garden slowly but surely, he was well aware of his endowment and didn't want to hurt her, for she would have most certainly engaged her omen, leaving him a mindless slave till his death. He gently pushed it in, gradually going deeper and deeper with every stroke, increasing momentum and vigour. He was aiming for the roof of her womanhood, precisely why he put the pillows on her back to make that difficult spot to reach, that drives women mad with pleasure and most men believe to be a myth, accessible to him.

Her eyes were wide open and mouth ajar in disbelief as he stroked her spot with laser precision to a point that she felt him in her belly. He rocked and thrusted, alternating between great speed and slow long strokes and great speed again. Her legs trembled. She ran out of breath. He slowed down while running his thumb on the top part of her entry point, giving it a massage and gently applying pressure on it.

"OH YES!!!" she yelled as he stroked even harder with his collar on, all while skilfully working his thumb until she pushed him away and sprayed a fountain of love fluid in the air that came dripping down the bed as nectar rain.

He was still rock-hard but knew if he did any more, she would perceive him as a sadistic person that enjoyed her pain. He lay next to her, having have gotten her as close to nirvana as she had ever been. He held her tight and joined her in slumber.

Jessica, Genevieve's assistant, had been working in the office late and came home tired, lonely, and hungry. She showered and fixed herself something to eat. Her cat came to disrupt her meal, as they are known to do. She cut off a piece of her sandwich and tossed it across the room so it would leave her alone for a while. She lived at the top floor of an apartment in a rough neighbourhood. It was hard to meet anyone decent in her immediate environment, but at least she had a spectacular view of Clarence City from her living room.

She made her way to the window with a mug of coffee and stared at the bright city lights and apartment buildings that still had their lights on despite the odd hours of the night. 'I wonder how many people are locked in a tight embrace and having orgasms tonight while I'm here at my sexual peak and alone with my cat.'

She could feel the frustration creeping up to her. She shut the blinds and walked to a closet that was in her bathroom and came out with a box wrapped in a beige gift paper. Her college friend who had gone to Thailand on vacation noticed her lack of sexual activity and got her a gift from one of the globally renowned sex shops in Bangkok.

Tonight, she would get hers even if it meant that she would engineer it herself. She pulled out the device that required deep insertion to get pleasure. The instructions were in mandarin and hers was a bit rusty…probably why she missed the warning sign on the box that laid caution on the machine's extreme vibration capabilities. It came with a controller that had an adjustable dial that could manipulate the machine to provide vibrations in low, medium, and high intensities. She slipped it in over her colourful pyjamas and set it at low as she caressed her bosoms, flicking her right milk raisin with her index finger as she started to enjoy the feeling. It vibrated at precise areas of her womanhood that left her biting her lip.

She set it at medium and could feel the vibrations down her spine. 'Powerful for a tiny device,' she thought as she started to get a mild orgasm and twisted the knob too high for a grand finale when all hell broke loose and she was in serious danger of having a life-threatening completion! She reached in and pulled it out as she convulsed for a fair five minutes, having multiple eruptions one after the other that engaged her whole body. Her pyjamas were ruined, so she took them off and jumped in the bed nude to turn in for the night after experiencing *Le petite Mort*: 'the small death,' a term the French used to describe an eruption of a sexual nature.

Chapter XIII
The Loyalty and Treachery Curve

In a world of balance and *yin yang*, loyalty brewed just as its direct counterweight that is terrible treachery formed in the shadows. Dionysus's vow of servitude to Genevieve would eventually be her saving grace and the scheming plot of betrayal from the Moretti family under Don Gianni, her fly in the ointment as well as John's certain doom.

Dionysus had been formally inducted into the affairs of her work life as well as those of a personal and intimate nature in order to have him as a complete asset. She bore all to him and came clean about her current predicaments, accomplishments, and how she acquired them, granting him unfettered access and sparing no detail.

He was fully aware that she used her abilities to sway the late mayor to granting her company the contract to change the entire city skyline with her futuristic building designs and was in utter shock of how efficient her curse was on men who fell victim to it. He considered himself a special case that he had seen nirvana between her thighs several times over since the first time and was of sound mind.

He was under her employ as personal adviser and bodyguard, a position that raised a few eyebrows in the office, seeing how he made a five-figure salary for what to the untrained eye would appear as redundant work. He had met John, Jessica, and the entire board as he attended several board meetings and silently sat, listening and assessing the progress that they were making, jotting down points of merit and limitations brought up by board members in public while in private, he was assisting Genevieve with decision-making as he would weigh in as a voice of reason and strategic approaches that served her best interest and kept her anonymity intact, all while running security measures that would keep her safe. He was truly a far cry from the troubled priest he once was.

John's meeting with the family had paid off. The FFC was making good progress, uninterrupted by the mob affairs and with the full support of the community as they put up structures in a matter of months, leaving their laborers working tirelessly but handsomely compensated for their woes, achieving feats like completing a few of the buildings in key areas. He attended many family gatherings after the first. He even began to enjoy the festivities, as his relationship with Jacklyn remained restricted to hotel rooms in neighbouring towns and secret knocks at his door at odd hours. Dionysus had wondered how he managed to acquire an audience with the mob kingpin that most of the city couldn't identify, so he ran an investigation, secretly following him as he went to family gatherings and rendezvous with Jacklyn, gathering photographic evidence and giving Genevieve a detailed brief on his discoveries. He was truly an asset and a great companion.

The Moretti family had fallen to some hard times. The newly appointed mayor was on a war-path and hell bent on bringing down the mob. He had a personal vendetta, as they had sent a lot of his colleagues to an impromptu grave from his days as a police officer. He had managed to identify two of the four dons and even pulled off tying Don Castillo to human-trafficking charges, one that he couldn't execute without the help of Mai Lin, a high-ranking Southeast Asian madam under the mob's employee that would help manage the working girls and break language barriers. She gave up his whole operation in exchange for money, citizenship, and protection, providing locations on brothels and a shipment from Vietnam of kidnapped girls that was to arrive and be inspected by Don Castillo in the flesh. He was arrested at the port, caught in the act, and indicted with human-trafficking charges that would see him age and die in prison, a punishment that fit the crime.

The second person on his radar was Don Salvatore. He had foiled a few of his operations but he was too vigilant to be tied to any of the crimes. He did, however, manage to arrest some of his top-ranking generals in two operations. The first was a sting operation they called tainted barrel. The Salvatore mob would research employees working in local Bourbon distilleries, buy their services, and inspire their loyalty whenever they had plans to renege on their arrangement by threats to them and theirs. For the last decade, they had stolen fifty bottles from every barrel that held one hundred and fifty bottles of premium bourbon and rye whiskey. They would blame the variance in harvest on 'angel's share' or 'drink for the angels,' which are terms used casually to define the quantity of alcohol that evaporates in barrels, while in aging process, that typically adds up to over thirty percent of the barrel's content. In some rare cases, depending on storage and gestation period, angel's share would account up to fifty percent. The inconsistency was the grey area that they flourished in.

Someone on their payroll would collect cases of the unaccounted precious elixir in a truck, delivering them to a warehouse storage where they would later sell them to some unsuspecting liquor store distributors at retail price. It was a brilliant source of revenue until one of the distillery owners saw bottles of a limited-edition batch that he thought he was the only individual in possession of at the Moon Crystal Bar and Restaurant while drinking at the bar counter.

He smelled a fish and secretly procured the services of a logistics company to run down semantics that surely led to the scandal coming to light. He involved the authorities who then let the operation run a bit longer in hopes that the don would eventually rear his head to check on the operational details but he never did. They eventually had to shut down the honey trap and arrest the culprits who were already positively identified and tied to the Moretti mob, offering lighter sentences in hopes that they would testify against the top brass of the crime faction. Naturally, they wouldn't dare give up the don's details, for it was unhealthy, counter-self-preservative, and could easily result in a contagious outbreak of lead poisoning that would spread in their household and infect their wives, children, and loved ones, as brutal as the Morreti mob wrath was ,, sometimes even their victims pets .

The second was Operation Cash Cow, of which they came within shaving distance of finally arresting him, but he slithered out of their grasp like grabbing a fish in the water. They had noticed a strain of murders in the city, of which the victims were young, beautiful, barely legal college girls with unexplained assets, cash flow, and fancy cars. The explanation to where they got the possessions according to investigation reports from friends and surviving family was that they had generous lovers.

Upon further investigation, they found out that these girls had huge life-insurance policies taken on them, paid by their alleged generous lovers who were also members of the Salvatore mob and would buy them apartments, cars, and give them a high five-figure monthly entertainment allowance, taking a life insurance on them and masking it as affection. The girls would perceive them as cash cows until they would mysteriously die, leaving a huge sum of money to be collected by the 'grieving' generous lovers. The funds would go to the mob. Their more lucrative, if not most malicious, revenue-generating activities and one the don was about to engage in until his informant in the taskforce warned him that they were closing in on him. He cut off all ties with the lady that would have been his victim, leaving her with the possessions he had gotten for her and the authorities stumped at his elusiveness.

Mayor Claude was a force of nature, a cosmic response to the brutality of the mob that spread like an oil spill in the ocean and went unchecked till the universe set him loose on them. If they slipped up, he would be the one to deliver the finishing blow. His biggest challenge was pinpointing who was at the head of the Moretti family, as no one would give him up and feared him or in the spirit of gender equality, her more than spending a lifetime in prison.

With the mob under attack from the authorities, they needed a way to make their revenue streams justifiable should there be any question on the legitimacy of their assets. As payment of cooperating with FFC, Genevieve and the FFC agreed to give the Moretti family a six-story building in the down skirts of town, of which he had designs to build some high-end retail stores of expensive suits, jewelleries, and watches, a bar at the rooftop, and an entire building that he would use to run his ill-gotten funds through to make his earning justifiable.

The work was complete and the building operational, serving its purpose as a six-story washing machine, of which the mob would 'clean' its money. He met with the remaining mob bosses and discussed the troubling times. The building was undeniably a good idea, as they moved their funds right in front of the law's all-seeing eye, none the wiser, a perfect loophole. They did, however, desire more property and decided to approach Genevieve on getting a building in every zone in the city that would serve as their base of operation and turf strong hold.

Don Giani made his way to the FFC tower chest out, for no one of sound mind dared deny him. He had what his psychiatrist growing up called a Viking complex. He was prone to violence and carried the delusion that he could take whatever he wanted and whenever he wanted it. That explained his career path. One wondered the vindication the psychiatrist that gave that small boy's psychological assessment would feel on seeing the terrible man he would grow up to be.

The valet opened the door for him as he walked through the lobby and then stopped to take in the view of the centrepiece, the sculpture of the tree Genevieve grew up looking at and the serpent hanging from its branches. He wasn't aware of the story behind it. He just appreciated the craftsmanship. Commotion disrupted his daze and he moved along, walking with purpose and looking down on the regular folk breaking their backs for a monthly wage of about the same price of the bottle of Brunnelo Monti he had for lunch. 'Fools! I If they can't get rich in such a big playground as Clarence City, then they deserve to be overworked and underappreciated,' he thought as he walked past the miserable bunch with a smug face that the oblivious employees that crossed paths with him assumed was a smile and responded in such to the perceived gesture, which made him even more perplexed. 'What a bunch of happy sheep!' he thought to himself as he made his way to the elevator and was slingshot to the very top of the tower where Genevieve's office was based.

He walked in unannounced and under the impression that the element of surprise would improve his chances of getting her to agree to his demands, evidence that he was lacking in foresight and didn't fully understand who he was dealing with, for if he did, he wouldn't have set in motion events that would lead to his ruin.

She was in the process of drawing up last-minute additions to a building design with the help of an artist and Jessica beside her, shadowing her as she was now under her mentorship, undoubtedly the physical manifestation of the fondness she had for her.

"We need to talk." He walked in, inviting himself to the comfortable chair on the client end of her desk. "Sit. Why don't you?" He ignored her sarcasm in favour of getting straight to business. "Give us the room," she instructed the rest of the occupants in her office and they cleared out quicker than they would if the fire alarms were going off and evacuations were in progress.

"What brings you to my office?" she asked while looking into his eyes, the windows to one's soul serving as an accurate description of her philosophy, for she could tell a lot by looking into a man's eyes and trusted her assessment from them more than facial expressions, and his were those of a drowning man willing to latch on, climb on, and step on anyone in the pool of misery with him to stay afloat. The smug on his face was a practiced facade to hide his urgency. He wasn't at her desk to show gratitude for her generosity or to discuss mutually beneficial ventures but rather to a strong arm and renegotiate on initial arrangements.

"I want to renegotiate our terms. I would involve John, the bridge between us, but the sensitivity of this matter demanded a personal touch over that of a liaison." His proposition was predictable. She had seen this dance countless of times. His next step would be to make an impossible ask that she would deny and he would result in a show of dominance and intimidation. She yawned in terrible boredom as her educated guess started to unravel before her eyes.

"The building you gave as payment for the Moretti family's blessing has been such a great asset to us… to the extent that we would like to acquire more."

"You mean procure," she rephrased the statement and interrupted him while he spoke.

"To the extent that we would like to 'acquire' more," he repeated his statement, emphasising on the word 'acquire' by prolonging its pronunciation and changing its natural intonation, suggesting he meant what he said and didn't need correction, on the same token implying that he wasn't planning on following traditional rules of commerce that would entail compensating the FFC on the buildings he intended to acquire.

"My designs are all spoken for and in high demand. Getting you the building in your possession was a hard-enough task. I suggest you take it for what it is, an overcompensation to buy your security and silence on our arrangement. If anything, you should leave my office content!" She was growing impatient and needed to get to the point of impasse that this encounter would eventually end in. The don looked at her in disbelief of her audacity.

"I expect such arrogance from someone who is oblivious of my dealings and doesn't know who I am by night, not from a well-informed perceptive bitch like you. Saying no to me is highly unwise, unless you enjoy permanent deep-sea diving or shallow graves." He didn't know it yet but he had uttered the words that would hammer the last nail to his coffin.

"Since you came in here making threats, I'll make one of my own, cease and desist, or I'll unleash a hellish wrath on you that will shatter your feeble world into pieces and burn what's left to ashes," she responded in a nonchalant, unperturbed-by-his-valid-threats type of tone that he found unsettling. She either didn't care about the consequences or had a death wish. He stood up, adjusted his parasols, and she remained seated, leaning back on her chair as they exchanged aggressive stares. He turned away and stormed towards the exit. He held the doorknob and came to a halt before opening it and walking through. He looked back at her. "Stay safe. These are dangerous times." He shut the door behind him and walked towards the elevator.

Genevieve had walked a few paces behind him to make certain he would leave from her domain, like a viscous serpent hissing and rattling, advancing towards a perceived threat until it would leave its territory. Her omen was itching to get out. She could feel her alter ego clawing from under her skin. The elevator door opened and he got in, but before the automatic doors shut, he caught a glimpse of her second form, her serpent-like eyes looking back at him! As the lift deescalated, he debated on the facts of the terrifying sight, and by the time the elevator doors opened and he exited towards the lobby, he had come to the conclusion that what he saw briefly was but a trick from the room's light reflection, although he still couldn't shake the feeling that it wasn't an optical illusion.

Dionysus was at the parking lot when the verbal altercation occurred. She was glad that she had sent him out of the office, for had he been present, it would mean trouble for her and the Moretti family, for they would be having a funeral, while Dionysus and her would be co-conspirators in a murder charge.

He flung through the door hurriedly, as office gossip had reached him that a man was in her office causing a ruckus. He walked towards her table where she was seated as calm as a lake that could pass for a mirror. "I saw Giani's car leave from the lot as I was coming in… What did he want?"

She looked back at him and ominously responded, "War!"

Chapter XIV
Drapaeu De Guerrre
'Flags of War'

Coin Flip Tails

Lines had been drawn in the sand. She let the Moretti family keep the building, for she never once went back on a deal spoken or signed. She, however, assumed that Giani would consider mutual destruction as reason to keep clear, for if he made an attempt towards her life and failed, she would alert the authorities of his dealings and expose his identity.

She went on for months without as much a death threat when one day she was picked up by a chauffeur she had never been driven by before. Upon inquiring the whereabouts of her regular one, he informed her that he was feeling under the weather and he was his replacement until he was fit to work. They were stuck in rush-hour traffic when he shut the partition and exited the car, disappearing in the crowd. She tried to push the doors open but they were shut from the central-locking system. The windows wouldn't badge or break either. A hissing sound came from the left car seat and the smell of bitter almonds filled the car soon after. She recognised the scent and grabbed the Swiss Army knife that she carried in her purse not because she needed it for personal protection purposes but because it could one day prove useful like in such a situation. She tore through the seat to confirm her suspicions. The hissing sound came from a gas canister attached to a release mechanism and a mobile phone that served as a remote trigger. The gas was undoubtedly cyanide. She folded the knife, put it back in her purse, opened the limo car fridge, pulled out a bottle of champagne and a crystal champagne flute, popped it open, and poured herself a glass. Part of her arrangement with the dark entity from her vision and that she would later come to discover was that she could never die from the hands of an enemy. She sipped her champagne and began to laugh at her own humour. "I love the smell of cyanide in the morning," she said as she inhaled the toxic gas. One who couldn't see the full spectrum would assume that she had a terrible fight-or-flight reaction to imminent danger, as anyone in her position would be screaming and yelling for help.

If cut, she bled like a normal person but with a guaranteed recovery in an almost mediocre human timeframe that left no scars, blemishes, or permanent damage to her organs regardless of how deep the cut. The cars behind her honked as angry drivers yelled words of profanity, for her chauffeur-less car was holding off traffic. The noise turned to an inaudible commotion and slowly evolved into a high-pitch frequency ring in her ears, fading to complete silence as her vision cut to black and she lost consciousness.

When she came to, he was seated next to her hospital bed asleep, maintaining the look of concern as he went to the land of Ned. Her room was well decorated with get-well-soon gifts, flowers, and well-wishers' paraphernalia, such as baskets of pastries and boxes of expensive chocolates that came from far and beyond in lands where boxes of chocolates were ridiculously expensive. "Is it Monday already?" she jokingly asked, playfully suggesting the gifts that filled up her room were a normal and ordinary routine for a Monday morning. He woke out of his slumber and had already processed that she was awake. In the army, they were trained to sleep lightly and over the explosive sounds of mortar fire. He admittedly had a better night's rest at the warzones than on that hospital chair, for he knew he had failed her and broken his vow of servitude by letting harm come to her in form of an assassination attempt that by all means and purposes should have succeeded. There was enough cyanide in that canister to kill an entire ballroom... full of elephants! He embraced her and gave her a hand as she stood up.

"How long have I been out?" she asked, surprisingly full of beans as she ripped the drip needles out of her arm, pulled out the hospital tag that was on her left hand, and stripped from the hospital gown, exposing her complete nude, grabbing a fresh outfit that Dionysus had brought for her in hospital, praying and hoping she would wake up with her usual spring in step and *joie de vivre*, of which his prayers were answered. She turned back at him and gave him a seductive look as she stood on her tiptoes and provocatively swayed her hips while slipping on the yellow summer dress. It wasn't her style or her colour but she knew the media were camping outside, awaiting the doctor's final word and her walking out through the backdoor , her normal power suit getup would make her an easy target to spot. She admired his detail and foresight to think all that through.

She walked towards him to kiss him and put him at ease that she was never in any real danger. Her read on him was that he was beating himself up for not being there when she needed him the most. "I can't die at the hands of an enemy." It was a fact she had failed to mention and was planning on keeping it to herself until he was ready to carry such privileged information of her female equivalent to an Achilles heel, circumstances and his unrelenting loyalty led her to hasten to the conclusion that he was.

"If you were to grab the scalpel behind me and cut out my beating heart, I'm nearly certain I wouldn't survive. You are the only person in the world capable of doing so." His chest tightened as his heart grew larger and he leaned over to kiss her. He was hers! Doctors rushing in interrupted their intimate moment dropped their clipboards and jaws alike upon seeing her on her own two feet.

"Mrs. Henrietta, I wouldn't recommend you to be on your feet." One of the doctors rushed towards her to assist her back to her bed. He was met with great hostility as she shoved him back.

"I feel just fine and shall be exiting the hospital as soon as possible," she responded in an authoritative manner that no one in her immediate surroundings dared defy.

"That's fine but allow us to at least run some tests before you leave. The amount of gas you inhaled would have killed you on the spot, let alone being considered impossible to recover from," the physician expressed his concerns.

"I guess I have a guardian angel." She looked at Dionysus with a look of content and turned back to address the doctor.

"I'll skip any further medical probing, and to clear you of all complaisance, I'll sign the waver that claims I left the hospital on my own volition and against medical advice. Then I shall be on my way." He was impressed that she was well versed in the due process of medical bureaucracy. She had been a war nurse in a previous life.

"Since I can't convince you to stay, here is my card. Please contact me should you change your mind and heed my strong advice to remain admitted in hospital. He gave her the card and waiver that she singed even without going through the fine print. They soon after made it to the back exit where a new Lincoln Town Car was waiting for her. Dionysus had assumed the role of chauffeur till he found and thoroughly vetted one. She wasn't about to let him drive her around while she sat at the back so she sat at the front passenger seat.

"Haven't ridden shotgun in a while." She appreciated the change of scenery and the company even more.

They took a moment before beginning the journey to take advantage of the silence and privacy in the car. She noticed his bruised knuckles and straight deep cuts on his palms as he rested his hands on the steering wheel. "So what have you found out?" she asked, the answer to which she could speculate to and end up with an accurate identification of who had hired the man who carried out the attempt. "I found CCTV footage of the assassin impersonating your chauffeur, abandoning the car in traffic after setting off the gas release mechanism in the car… He was quite good. He soon after evaded the cameras by taking the tunnel and subway... I then spotted someone who fit his description but in an entirely new outfit exiting the subway in East Clarence City where he checked into the ambassador suite room 1521 of the Dukes and Duchesses Hotel.

His vigilance was incomparable. He had managed to track him down a few feet of his precise location. Even the authorities hadn't begun, nor did they know where to start. His talents were truly being wasted as a priest.

"I soon after paid him a visit where a physical altercation ensued upon my arrival. He was too good a fighter and probably had a hefty price for his services. I managed to subdue him and get some information out of him... to an extent." She was surprised at how efficient and good at his job he was. The bruises on his fists were obviously from punches thrown at the culprit's dental formula. The wire cuts were something she had seen before on a person who had recently used a fibber wire as a garrotte... that he sat beside her with but superficial injuries visible to only those kin of vision was a testament to his skill, that he was at her bedside only after avenging her, and identifying all the parties involved in the attempt on her life was tribute to his loyalty. She was certain she made the right decision by telling him her Achilles heel.

"Care to take a wild guess who ordered the hit?" he asked sarcastically, fully aware that they both had the same person in mind. They said it together, risking the jinx god's wrath. "Giani Moretti!" He started the engine and drove off, heading to her penthouse where they turned in for the night.

Don Giani was in state of panic but hid it well to the people in the room. News of her miraculous recovery and hospital discharge cut him like a double-edged sword. He would have called the man he paid to do the wet work but the fact that he hadn't heard from him meant he was either dead or in custody, telling the authorities all his secrets in exchange for a lighter sentence.

He discussed his woes with Don Salvatore who was a known master strategist in mob affairs as well as crisis management in hopes his evil-scheming ingenious mind would adapt to his conditions and provide an impromptu action plan that would work out much like an improvised play by ear violinist's vibrato.

After much brainstorming, he settled on two options on his next course of action. The first was of a counter-intuitive nature and would have passed as a deranged tongue twister while saying aloud and repeatedly, "Hiring an assassin to kill an assassin for a failed assassination." The second was reaching out to Genevieve through John as designated intermediary to patch fences and bury the hatchet if she would accept his olive branch, a bitter pill to swallow but one he would easily ingest in exchange of freedom from incarceration. He summoned John to his estate.

He was lying in the bed with her, soaking in post coital endorphins when he got the text on the cell phone that the don gave to all high-ranking members of the family to be the preferred communication apparatus when discussing mob-related business on the phone. *"State of emergency declared come to the estate ASAP."* He typically wouldn't respond instantly to his beck and call but knowing the challenges with authorities they were facing lately, he excused himself and explained that he had a family emergency and had to leave right away. Her heart broke just a little, for she knew for him to leave her naked in bed and eager to indulge in certain physical activities multiple times, he must have been involved with the mob deeper than she anticipated. She watched him hastily dress up and leave. The door shut and she burst into tears, wishing with all her being that she would have listened to her gut and cut ties with him as soon as he told her who he was. She considered herself a strong character and hadn't cried in years. It was then Jacklyn realised that she had fallen in love with him. His troubles were now hers and she was complicit.

John instructed the chauffeur to drive him to the estate pronto. There was a van that was blocking the driveway, so he honked and aggressively used shooing gestures, letting the driver of the obstructing vehicle know that he needed to move out of his way quicker than a bat out of hell. He then proceeded to stomp the gas pedal as he craftily manipulated the steering wheel, taking every apex in corners and blowing through-speed limits.

John reached for his backseat compartment and pulled out a firearm. A company in Clarence City had developed a concealable nine-millimetre pistol that could fold into half and appear as unimposing as a smartphone in his pocket until he would pull it out and unfold it locked and loaded, thanks to its self-loading mechanism.

They were soon at the estate and he rushed in, his hands unassumingly in his pockets clutching his concealed weapon, alert and priming his reflexes should he be required to use it in a helter-skelter fashion. The don hadn't explained the nature of the emergency that made him reach out at such odd hours of the night and he couldn't help but feel that he was walking into an ambush.

The smell of cigar smoke had made its way to the parking lot. He followed it and it naturally led him to the round table at the porch Don Salvatore and Giani were seated. "Perfect timing," he commended him for his punctuality as he reached for the empty seat to complete the round-table mob trio.

"Awfully comfortable for a state of emergency." His witty remark was soon ignored as grave facial expressions dictated that they had their fill of formalities.

"The day of reckoning is closing in by the minute," Giani began to explain his predicament. "My informant in the force tells me Mayor Claude and his band of self-righteous lawmen have tied the Moon Crystal as a family asset and are operating surveillance to identify who runs the place. It goes without saying that we need to steer clear of the place, managing it from afar unless you want to put them on your radar." He looked at John, suggesting that he was addressing him, since that ship had sailed for Don Salvatore.

"To add to our woes, I had a direct dealing with that fancy bitch CEO of yours." He paused to look at his natural reaction after he dropped breadcrumbs insinuating that he was responsible for the attempt on her life. It took him a moment to piece together what he was tipping the wink.

"What did you do?" John gave him a grim look and he was momentarily tempted to pull out his gun and empty the chamber towards the occupants of the table, ridding the world of a terrible cancer in doing so.

Don Giani picked up on his resentful tone in his response-deserving question that he arrogantly remained quiet to as if it were rhetorical. "This is a call to arms, not a social invite. You kissed the ring and pledged loyalty to the family turning back on that can have some serious consequences." He paused again to let him process and decide, for he had noticed John's hand slowly reaching for his right pocket. He pondered quietly before he loosened the grip on the pistol in his coat after thinking of what the consequences might entail if he put a bullet through his dome. "I watched you grow up. You were a smart boy and we all knew you were going to accomplish great things when you grew up. However brilliant you were, I could tell that you didn't have a certain quality Moretti heirs have in you. You avoided confrontation, abhorred violence, and was squeamish to the sight of blood till you were in your early twenties. As a child, you went to a school trip to a farm and watched sheep getting slaughtered and decided you wouldn't eat meat for years. I was possibly the first person to realise that you had the linage but not the grit, and if not properly monitored, you would give up or betray the family when a little pressure was applied... I figured since you would cave under pressure, I would use your weakness in my favour." He pulled out his phone and showed him live footage of Jacklyn tied up, beaten black and blue in a place that looked industrial in the background of the shaky footage.

"She is loyal to a fault and wouldn't tell us anything about you even when we tried to get it out of her." He continued, "What do you want?" he asked in complete emotional anguish.

"Well, Johnny boy, I want you to smooth things over between your lady boss and the family. Drop her guard. Only then will I have her pushing up daisies like a florist. Then you shall use your influence in the company to secure us some moderately sized buildings of her designs in key turf regions of the city, which will serve as proxies to legitimise our funds. Do you think you can handle that simple task or shall I tell the boys to run a train on her till she is paralysed from the waist down?" Rage burned inside him like the great fire of Rome but he maintained composure for the sake of her safety, a notion in which he mastered a courage he never knew he was capable of bringing him to the conclusion that he was hers. He accepted his terms. "She shall be back in your arms after you follow and complete my instructions. I'll have the boys make her comfortable. Until then, she shall not want anything... but her freedom."

Chapter XV
Drapaeu De Guerrre
Flags of War

Coin Flip Heads

Jacklyn was on her bed crying over John's hasty exit from an intimate moment that made her feel underappreciated as well as made her face facts that she had developed deep feeling towards him. She typically wouldn't tolerate or maintain a relationship with any man who would assume her to that degree. She thought herself weak of will to set out the governing boundaries of her casual relationship with John, only to be the one to breach them by falling in love. "No wonder he would just get up and leave to a 'family emergency' that required no further explanation. I taught him to treat me that way," she said engaging in a self-loathing monolog. She shut her eyes to sleep off her misery when her door was kicked in and masked men dragged her out of her bed like an alarm clock on a school night. They carried her away as she bit, clawed, and kicked, attempting to slip from their grasp but all attempts in vain as she was shoved in the blue van that was parked at the driveway all evening, obstructing John's chauffeur as he tried to rush him to the Moretti Estate. It turned out the don summoned him to get him out of the house so as to abduct her and have her camera ready as leverage for his proposition, a true master of his dark trade.

Dionysus had procured a small arsenal and a replacement chauffeur. He left Genevieve in her penthouse under a protective detail as the authorities paid her visit after visit, asking for detailed accounts of what transpired in the vehicle. They also asked her follow-up questions about the perpetrator, for they had found the body of a man at the Dukes and Duchesses Hotel's ambassador suite who appeared to have been beaten to a pulp, tortured and finished off by garrotte strangulation. "Who would want you dead?" they asked.

"Who wouldn't?" She gave a vague, cryptic answer, expressing that she had a lot of enemies that would make an attempt on her life , she was playing coy that she was oblivious about the identity of the culprits.

They soon left, leaving her in peace and scheming on how she could lure Don Giani to her where she would introduce him to her omen. She had given Dionysus strict instructions that he was not to be harmed by his hand. She did, however, fail to mention the rest of the Moretti's as off-limit targets.

He knew where they took refuge, the Moretti Estate, as he had followed John there several times. In his massive, oddly shaped bag was a sniper rifle that he had modified down to the *T* to resemble his service weapon from lock stock and barrel. He favoured a monolithic suppressor over a muzzle break that counter-recoils the gun flick from an upward motion to a downward one. His barrel was crafted to increase bullet velocity and range ,an extended magazine, attached to the camouflaged, painted riffle that allowed him to fire twenty rounds without reloading over a hairpin trigger that responded to the touch of his finger quicker than Genevieve's dew-filled lady garden.

When Nathan died, Dionysus dismounted the SIG Sauer scope-four optic on his rifle and sling. They would serve as mementos until recently when he decided to go hunting for Moretti. Hiding in a thicket, he mounted his weapon and looked through its optical. Through it, he saw Don Giani smoke a cigar at the porch with Don Salvatore as John approached. He watched the collective through his sights as things went from cordial to heated. He noticed John reaching for his right coat pocket whenever he appeared threatened, suggesting that he was carrying some kind of concealable weapon. That would be problematic for him, as he would be forced to act quickly. "Don't do it," he whispered under his breath and took a sigh of relief when John talked himself out of his intended course of action.

Genevieve had reserved Don Giani for her omen. John was playing both sides and by the look of things didn't care much for the Moretti family anymore, leaving Don Salvatore as the only target and selected recipient of a well-deserved bullet in dome. He decided to let things play out as he watched from a far in a thicket fairly five hundred yards out and with a great flied of view of the table. He watched Giani hand John a cell phone and watched his face turn blue in terror after watching what he assumed was a footage of some kind, for he looked at the phone for some time without touching its screen.

He couldn't make out what they were saying but he had a working assumption that Don Moretti had found leverage of sorts and was showing John evidence of his possession of it on the phone he had handed to him. His reaction upon looking at the screen was of concern, not one of his wellbeing but one of a loved one, and having had personally met the man and spied on him in his natural habitat, he speculated that there was only one person who would warrant such a reaction from John, the journalist girl he had been secretly seeing, Jacklyn Serabona.

He briefly considered adding John to his list of bullet recipients, for if Jacklyn had been kidnapped by Don Moretti in order to force his hand to betray Genevieve, he must have been convinced it would work. He then reconsidered when the idea to use the fact that they weren't aware that he had figured out their treacherous plot came to him.

Their meeting was concluding and he had selected his target. It was fairly dark where he was hidden but the table at the porch was well lit. He could see them, while all they saw was pitch-darkness. With Don Salvatore in his sights, he began doing the calculations in his mind on how he would deal his fatal shot.

It was quite a windy night. This would greatly affect bullet trajectory but he was an excellent marksman. Ten-minute-per-hour winds were blowing from seven o'clock to one o'clock, from his back left to his front right. That meant that he would have to adjust his scope for half value winds that would be five minutes per hour. Had the wind been hitting his face or back, that would have been a no-wind value assessment. He adjusted accordingly, considering parallax and minute of angles at one click, something most snipers couldn't manage to do without a spotter. He took slow and deep breaths to slow his heart rate and finally held his breath to steady his shot, pulling the trigger and ridding the world from the grip of terror this terrible man had on it in doing so.

The kickback from his rifle shook his entire torso as the muzzle flashed and Don Salvatore fell to the floor, making a thud, a huge chunk of his face blown to smithereens and blood and brain matter splattered in a ten-yard radius.

John and Giani ducked for cover, both pulling out their concealed firearms and returning fire at the direction they figured the shots were coming from, a far cry away from their actual target. Dionysus had already made a quick exit from the premises by vaulting over a nearby wall and sprinting to his motorcycle where he soon rode off at objective complete, he was trained to never go into enemy territory without an exit strategy and his was perfectly executed.

They emptied out their pistols, blindly firing in the dark and hoping that the sniper would pick up a stray projectile, they waited for a while and came to the conclusion that whoever was responsible was either injured or had escaped, since no more shots had been fired from his end. They both rushed to Don Salvatore's aid only to find him dead on the floor, oozing blood and barely recognizable from injuries acquired. John got sick at a nearby bush at the disturbing sight as Don Giani paced around in a state of panic, processing what had transpired. The Moretti throne now lay heavy on the head of Don Moretti without his foremost right-hand man, champion, and master strategist for he lay dead on the floor in a pool of his own blood.

Chapter XVI
Coupe De Grace

She was caught up with his transgressions as he confessed much like she did at that fateful afternoon when she spoke her truth. She intended to exact vengeance by her own hand at the group of deluded men who were way above their heads, assuming her as prey and not predator. He had taken the liberty to strike at the enemy without consulting her, feeding Don Moretti's paranoia and raising his guard by assassinating Don Salvatore. Yet, she couldn't stay upset with anyone who would care enough for her best interest to avenge her. His loyalty honoured her despite her scolding him for not involving her in the decision. "I'm truly sorry you feel that way but mine is to work in your best interests with or without your knowledge or consent," he explained his actions and gave her a detailed brief on the previous night's transgressions that entailed highlights of John working under duress for Don Moretti, a fact that she wasn't aware of and made her lessen the aggression of her scold.

John and Don Giani immediately took to the counter measures they had in store for such an occasion. Out of all the people who could carried out such an attack, very few would have the brass to carry it out. He could think of only one person who had the motive and resources to assassinate one of the dons: Genevieve. "This was vengeance," he speculated to John as they went indoors and shut the blinds for good measure just in case the sniper still had them in his sights.

"Whoever was behind that rifle was watching us for quite some time. He could have taken all of us out. I am guessing Don Salvatore was the desired target." They looked at each other as it dawned on them that the gunman wasn't trying to kill Giani but rather send him a message that he was not unreachable as well as causing the family some grief, presumably vengeance, for the attempted assassination of Genevieve.

The don composed himself and looked at John as if to set the mood back to the unsettling moment before shots were fired. "Set up the meet-up with your boss. I have a feeling she was responsible for this. If you choose to not comply, I'll consider you in cahoots with her and hold you partially responsible for the murder of Don Salvatore, a man who has done more for this family than you will ever know. You can guess what will happen next. I will set her free once you confirm the meet-up. Now leave before the authorities arrive and tie you to the family."

John hurriedly left the premises and arrived in his abode which had obvious signs of struggle, a busted lock, and broken coffee table. 'She did not go quietly,' he thought to himself as he nearly broke down in tears of distraught before quickly getting his composure. He had a huge task at hand of convincing Genevieve to meet with the person who presumably ordered an assassin to take her life.

He changed into a clean suit, one without bloodstains and made his way to the office earlier than he had ever done before. On his way up, he ran into Jessica who cordially greeted him. "You are here earlier than usual." She brought up the fact that he was off his routine timings. He nodded and smiled, giving her the impression that he was not in a talkative mood. She took it with a grain of salt and proceeded with her early-morning pre-work process that entailed a breakdown and compartmentalization of her to-do list in her mind. They were soon at the top floor, and for the first time in their whole career in FFC, Genevieve would be the one to greet them with coffee cups in hand when the elevator doors opened.

Jessica entertained the wildest notions of an alternate reality and flirted with the idea of metaphysical conceit, for the strangest thing had happened. She had her coffee brought to her by her boss and the tardiest person in the office was at work a fair two hours before his usual trimmings. "Take the day off. You have been really working hard lately," Genevieve told her as her eyes lit up in joyful surprise upon hearing that she would get an extra day to rest and get her affairs in order, the gesture adding to her speculative, ridiculous theory that the world was in retrograde and strange things would occur. "John Moretti and I will need to have a little chat." She called him by his family name as Jessica turned and got in the elevator. He didn't use the Moretti name for obvious reasons, the fact that she did confirm his suspicions that she knew more than she led on and might be the big bad wolf in sheep's clothing Don Moretti had assumed she was after all. The pair made their way to the privacy of her office. It would be the better part of two hours before the next person arrived for work. He sat on the client of her desk and she took her seat.

"I hear you have been keeping unsavoury company and dodging bullets by night," she said, confirming her involvement in last night's assassination, as news hadn't broken out about the shooting. "Cards on the table, I'll be candid and tell you most of what you probably know… I come from a top-brass Moretti bloodline. I had officially cut them off my life and their ways until you asked me to set up a meeting with them to obtain their blessing and cooperation while we broke ground and began rebuilding the city. We gave him a building but he demanded more as payment. He demanded my loyalty. Only then would he accept our terms. I kissed the ring and got back into the fold. Mine was to learn from the current don on operation matters and one day succeed him should he pass on. My involvement was minimal until last night when he summoned me to the Moretti Estate and kidnapped the woman I'm currently seeing before I even arrived at his doorstep. He admitted having had a falling out with you and in few words, he more or less took credit for your attempted assassination as a result of the argument you had…. He claimed that I needed motivation to work in the family's interest, so he used Jacklyn as leverage to coerce me into convincing you to meet at a location of your choice. I assume he wants to bury the hatchet but one can never trust such a person. That leaves me here at your desk, asking for your help. Please meet with him. Jacklyn's life depends on it."

She paused for a while before responding to his plea. "I'll do it. Inform the don I'm willing to meet. The location should be at my office as soon as he can… preferably before noon."

"Thank you!" John answered gratefully as he rushed to let the don know that she had accepted his term and that he should let Jacklyn go.

He used his special phone to contact him. "She accepted. Now please send me Jacklyn's location," he demanded impatiently.

"Well done, boy. You did well," the don responded and hung up his phone. John then received a text with GPS coordinates that he set in his car navigation and instructed his driver to hastily drive him to the location.

Dionysus walked in Genevieve's office. He was listening in from the intercom phone line in the other room. John's account's story matched with his working theory that the Moretti family wanted an audience with Genevieve but he strongly doubted their true intentions. She looked at him and smiled like she had never before.

"Hell awaits him," she said ominously. He found her eagerness to consume Giani's mind and soul unsettling but there couldn't have been anyone else more deserving of such a demise but the don.

"Give everyone working on this floor the day off. I shall be listening and watching from the other room, ready to spring into action should the need arise," he instructed her on the best laid out plan. She had finally found a person who could truly see her and today he would witness her omen in action.

Don Giani had escaped the compound before the authorities arrived so as to save his anonymity and not get listed as a known associate of the Moretti crime mob. The homicide detectives would arrive in the estate. After being notified of a shooting by one of the Moretti mob henchmen, they would classify the crime scene as a mob hit and sweep it under the rag, as they always did when members and leaders of any organised crime faction were done in. "They chose this life," a phrase they used to rationalised their lack of interest in solving mob-related murders.

Don Figiani had repatriated to Rome to expand on the European market, leaving Don Mingetti, his men, and his guns as the only ally to the Moretti mob. Giani had foreseen a war coming either with the authorities, with Genevieve, or the new player that was slowly but surely making advances towards the mob territory. He requested that his men be armed to the teeth with pistols, carbine rifles, and even grenades and plastic explosives, a tall order for anyone else but not for the Mingetti family, as they had ties with military generals who would skim from the inventory in Italy and various European countries as well as full control of the port where they would receive their stolen weapons. One of the men even had a javelin that shot service to air missiles capable of taking down a Boeing 747. If they decided to put their arsenal to use, Clarence City would have its darkest day and a graveyard over population issue.

Before his first altercation with Genevieve, he had a meeting with the leader of the rising faction that was noticeably pressing for specific areas of the Moretti turf. They met in an open field by the docks. His men were very intimidating and well organised. He could tell from how they ran security checks and the earpieces they used to communicate. 'A secure network is expensive in Clarence City. They clearly had resources,' he thought to himself.

What really stood out was the fact that they arrived moments before the don to clear the area of any perceived threats. They were well built and moved as a unit. He suspected that they were former military and had Arab features paired with uncanny accents that he deduced was Tunisian, as he had dealings with a Tunisian militia that made him aware of their distinctive features.

An average-built man with dark features walked out of a black SUV that drove towards the rendezvous after getting signalled that the area was secure. The men tensed and remained alert till he gave a subtle nod that would have passed for the cheekiest, barely noticeable command to be at ease. His eyes were those of a man who had taken countless lives. Giani could tell this, for he saw the same eyes every time he looked in the mirror.

"My name is Fulgar. I've come to your city not to take over your territory but to hunt. There is someone I have been tracking for quite some time and I believe she has taken refuge in Clarence City. We shall operate on the turf we have taken and shall leave once we have found who we are looking for. Do not take it upon yourself to go to war with us. It shall not bid well for you and yours. We can, however, be civil and work out compensation once I have found my target." He handed him his business card that read: *'FULGAR SECURITY SOLUTIONS, CEO and FOUNDER.'* He turned and walked back to his car as his men broke formation and snipers appeared in the most unassuming vantage points. Giani's men couldn't have picked up on their presence even if they knew where to look, a testament to their skill.

Upon seeking council with Don Salvatore moments before John arrived on the night he was shot, they decided to let Fulgar and his men operate, as war on three fronts would mean the certain fall of the Moretti family.

In the spirit of addressing the more pressing matters an t, he set course for the FFC tower to meet with Genevieve. He wasn't the least bit concerned that he was walking into an ambush for her choice in location implied that she was willing to negotiate. It would be much harder to commit murder in a building full of witnesses.

He arrived at the location of the GPS coordinates. His initial suspicion that she was kept in an industrial area was right as the coordinates led him to a warehouse located in a junkyard. He ran towards the door and kicked it open. The place seemed completely abandoned till he saw her in the furthest corner of the room, tied up to a chair. He ran as quickly as his feet could carry him towards her. The closer he got, the clearer the image of her current situation became. He realised that she was motionless and did not respond to him. Shouting her name at the top of his lungs, his heart pounded as he hyperventilated in fear of the worst. Her mouth was ajar. He grabbed her by her shoulders and shook her vigorously, hoping that she would come to, but her lips were chapped, her skin pale as the moon and cold to the touch, and her beautiful eyes had turned to a cloudy grey. He sobbed uncontrollably when it became clear to him that she was just an empty vessel. Jacklyn Serabona was dead!

In his grief, he attempted to pull her out of the chair she was bound in, and in doing so, he set off a pressure plate that was under her seat, setting off an explosive that could be heard ten miles out!

Genevieve's office windows vibrated from the citywide shockwave. She assumed it was a mild tremor as the don walked in with a despicable smirk on his face upon hearing the perceived tremor, for he knew what it truly was and what it meant, the faint sound of an explosion going off from a distance and that John Moretti and his undeclared lover had met their demise.

He walked in through the door with a different perspective than he had on their last encounter, for back then he thought of her as a weak-willed woman that could be easily strong-armed into doing his bidding. He had come to a very different conclusion, for she had survived his assassination attempt on her and managed to get her revenge within the course of the week. He obviously had underestimated her capabilities and resources, and for that, Don Salvatore paid the ultimate price.

Dionysus had set up a camera to monitor events unfold from the next room. Should things get heated or out of hand, he would hastily spring to action. She was going to use her omen on the unsuspecting don and he was going to watch her in action from a safe distance, for being in the same room could leave him under the sway. He knew that her omen only worked mid-coitus and understood that he would have to watch her get intimate with another man. He watched as she unbuttoned three buttons from her blouse before the don arrived. Blood rushed to his loins as she playfully took off her panties. She knew he was watching, fighting the urge to barge in and ravish her before the don arrived but the idea dawned on him too late, as the shockwave from perceived 'light tremors' destructed him from his erotic train of thoughts and a smug-faced Giani Moretti walked in.

"Have a seat," she instructed him and he followed.

"Well, quite the conundrum we find ourselves in," he stated the obvious and she looked back at him without uttering a word. He found the fact that she wasn't the least bit intimidated by him brain-racking. If only he knew how many encounters of a similar nature she had been in over time, he would have understood why she was nonchalant in such a tense moment. She had looked in the eyes of Barca of Carthage, Nero of Rome, and Napoleon of France as enemies and much more formidable adversaries than this misguided boy. She thought to herself as he processed his next words.

"I'm certain my nephew mentioned the purpose of my visit."

"Yes, that and much more," she responded, particularly to let him know that she was aware of the lengths he went to acquire an audience, also subtly hinting that she did not approve of his methods from the tone that she said it in. He chose to ignore the subliminal messages and proceeded to drive his proposition home.

"We are both fully aware what each other is capable of, although I must admit I was surprised to find out recently that there's more than meets the eye with you. The important thing is that we both recognise that we can be massive thorns on sides for each other should we go to war... I come offering peace, a ceasefire of sorts, and a vow to never meddle in your affairs only if you in exchange return the favour."

She held the idea in her mind and briefly considered, genuinely agreeing to his terms until she saw it, the glow of treason in his eyes. She had seen it in many men over the past, men who had ulterior motives of betrayal and ambitions of literary or figuratively stabbing knife in the back. The glow of treachery in his eyes was similar to that she saw in Giaya's Cassius before he pitted the senate against Caesar. It was the same glow she imagined Judas would have in his eyes when he betrayed the messiah.

"What guarantees do I have that you won't make a move against me when my guard is down and vice versa?" She addressed the obvious just to see his response and grade his sense of foresight as well as leading him to the page she wanted him to be at par with.

"Well, name your price. Perhaps a show of good faith from both parties can be a physical representation of our arrangement," he suggested.

"I have a better idea." She loosened another button from her shirt, exposing her stiff milk raisins that had a similar colour to a dark purple juicy grape. She put her feet up on the desk, the exact sequence of movements she performed with the late mayor. For the predator that she was, one would easily presume her office was her feeding ground. Giani's member throbbed, as he now knew precisely what was on her mind, and based on the empty office, he was certain that they were going to indulge in some intense sexual activities to seal their peace agreement. He stood up, walked to her, and unzipped his pants, pulling out his member that left much to be desired but had an average girth. She wasn't about to make Dionysus watch her pleasure another man with the lips he was so fond of kissing, she sprung out of her chair and performed a manoeuvre, leaving the don on the seat, his member erect and impressed by her agility. She patronisingly looked at him as she stepped on his left thigh with her Louboutin and gradually worked her hips to a mount positioning. She lifted her skirt and sat on his member. She could hardly feel it penetrate, as she was now accustomed to Dionysus's endowment. She turned the rotating chair to face the cameras, giving Dionysus a view of her and as little of the don as possible.

He was watching keenly as the moment built to its peak. His heart burned with rage when he saw him approach her and expose himself. He felt a fire in his loins when she manoeuvred and took the mount position and watched as she bounced up and down in rhythm.

He would join her in her escapades even if it meant that he would only get to do it from afar, unleashing the raging beast that was about to break the stitches from the confinement of his pants and gently started to stroke the tool of his anatomy that made her legs tremble in pleasure the night before. She could feel that he was enjoying the erotica from wherever he was watching the events unfold, so she looked at the hidden camera as she attempted to pleasure herself with the don before releasing her terrible omen.

He went for a good fifteen minutes before he was about to erupt and looked in her eyes, expecting the joy of release only to find the terrifying serpent eyes he thought he had hallucinated staring back at him. Uncanny, but it was almost as if they were looking into his soul. *"ANTE OMEN INFIRMATEM!"* she yelled as she had a small eruption. Dionysus finished with her from the other room and watched in pure shock as her omen was activated!

The don looked back at her, speechless, dazed, pale, and in pure terror of what was happening right in front of his eyes. She had never used the full power of her omen till today. Never had it been caught on camera either. The footage turned shaky and distorted. Dionysus could see what appeared to be brittle of sparks and ash dropping on the floor. "Call all your mob associates for dinner this evening, put up the most luxurious spread you can afford, and invite them over," she said in her hellish, terrifying voice and continued, "Rig the dinner table with enough plastic explosives to level a building and detonate just before dessert. Nod if you acknowledge." He nodded. *"Tu dismissed!"* She got off him and adjusted her attire accordingly as he slowly slipped off his euphoria and put his member away, exiting the office, cordially assuming he experienced *le petit mort*, unaware that through him she had just dealt the troubled mob, *a coup de grace*.

Later that evening, Dionysus and Genevieve sat at her office taking in the view of the city lights, enjoying each other's company but avoiding physical intimacy, for she still smelled like the don's aftershave when they heard a loud bang from the outskirts of the city that shook the building. They stared at each other, fully aware that Don Moretti had followed her instructions. "Second tremor today," he said sarcastically as she briefly made eye-contact and looked away. They continued consuming their whisky, knowing that possibly the entire Moretti lineage had been terminated in one swoop.

Chapter XVII
Fulgudr Percusserit Bis
'Lightning Strikes Twice'

She stood at the top of her domain, her buildings fully erect and testament to her vision and ambitions come to fruition. . It would only be a matter of time before the occupants of the physical manifestations of her architectural genius would take their due moving into the buildings she designed and taking a step into the future of infrastructure on the same tune. There were no hurdles that she could think of and no enemies that she could name seeing as how the entire Moretti mob was wiped out by her omen. However, she had lived a long life and had seen a pattern of no absolutes. That as much as she was an unstoppable force, there was someone, somewhere out there that would assume the role of an immovable object in her life. She would revel in the moment of one foot down till the other shoe would drop.

On seeing the footage of her omen, she realised similarities between the environment of her encounter with the dark entity and what her omen at full power made the room look like in the footage. The brittles of fire and ash could not have been caught by the naked eye and wouldn't have come to her attention were it not for the high-resolution hidden cameras Dionysus had planted in her office during her last encounter with the late don. It raised some concerns for Dionysus, for he had working assumption that he had caught a glimpse of hell but she was comfortable leaving it as the mysterious phenomenon it was.

The Morettis were long dead and buried and Fulgar and his men had begun to assume a takeover of turf but not of income-generating criminal activities. Prostitution, drugs, and illegal arms had come to an absolute standstill. The Moretti massacre as the media deemed it resulted in the drop of crime rate in Clarence City to a record low. For the longest time in a long time, Clarence City was flourishing in infrastructure and safety. The citizens didn't know it but they had Genevieve Henrietta to thank for both outcomes.

Fulgar and his men had procured a compound in the city outskirts where they trained with live weapons and a canine unit of Belgian Malinois in their menagerie. The late don was right in assuming their military background. Had he gone deeper into his research, he would have discovered that FULGAR SECURITY SOLUTIONS FSS was a Tunisian-based private security firm that had clients globally and was the go-to military contractor for the American government as well as other entities. Its ranks were full of highly decorated veterans and dishonourably discharged soldiers that had very unique skillsets, including a man who shot an insurgent from two miles away and was the personal advisor and right-hand man of Fulgar. He stood nearly seven feet tall, built like an ox, and had scars from a battle that entailed a very noticeable napalm burn on his left cheek: Cassim.

The band of brothers of FSS had fought wars in the world's hottest battlefronts for causes they did not care for nor believe in. "Fortune beats honour," would have sufficed for their embodied credo, for they lent their services undiscriminatingly to anyone who could afford them, mostly government factions that wanted to run a military operation discreetly, achieving their objectives without getting directly involved or being complaisant should the mission be compromised. With such a rap sheet, one would think that he was in Clarence City under employment but that would be a far cry from the truth. He was in the city on his own accord with but a few of his most trusted and most capable men as his entourage.

They worked under his orders to search for a woman of dark hair, unmatched beauty, and power, a woman who would strive for anonymity and had unexplained assets. He gave his vague instruction and his trusted men carried them out, embarking on a wild-goose chase of finding a needle in a haystack, searching for the better part of an year, slowly taking over key turfs from the Moretti family while running detailed surveillance and casual interrogations on the occupants within the perimeters. "Do you know of a beautiful woman nearby with unexplained wealth and in a position of power? She would be in the public eye yet not much about her would be known to the public…" They would ask to gather intelligence from shopkeepers, passers-by, and even to the extent of knocking on doors of unsuspecting residents only to be met with hostility and noncompliance, for if the mob era in Clarence City had taught its citizens anything, it was that a loose tongue led to a loose head.

It wasn't until Cassim came barging in Fulgar's home office with news of a discovery. "Sir, I think I found her."

Fulgar stood alert and immediately began to ask him follow-up questions. "How did you find her?" He was keen on knowing his methods to justify his end result.

"Sir, Channel Five was doing a feature on a woman called Genevieve Henrietta, detailing her gorgeous looks, her dislike of the spotlight, and achievements of her high-end buildings that would revolutionise infrastructure forever, making the city a hub for architectural advancements. Fulgar was certain that it was the woman he was looking for. Cassim handed him pictures of Genevieve and his face turned pale when he realised he was looking at the face of the woman he had searched the ends of the Earth to find!"

She looked different. Her hair was shorter and her visage as beautiful and young as he remembered based from all the variety of pictures in tabloids. She was every bit as ravishing as she had been if not more. Only this time, she went by the name Genevieve. "That's her!" He said in a shaky voice and his men had never seen him break a sweat even in the heat of battle. Anyone that could rattle Fulgar was to be approached with caution. "Wait for the right moment and bring her to me. Shut down all operations within the city and call everyone to the compound. We will soon host a very dangerous guest." He gave Cassim orders to put out the equivalent of a call to arms.

The mood in FFC was celebratory. Champagne flowed freely. They had accomplished quite the feat against all odds. A ribbon-cutting ceremony would be just around the corner. There was talk of her receiving a key to the city. Jessica had assumed the position of the late John Moretti and was now a fulltime partner and Genevieve's second in command. Dionysus's priorities had shifted from her fulltime protection detail to being by her side as treasured companion and ravishing her under silk sheets when the day was done. Had he kept his guard up, he would have been more security-conscious and noticed the black vehicle that tailed him every night as he and Genevieve made their way back to her penthouse or that the cleaners in FFC were not the same familiar faces he was accustomed to, rather Fulgar's men blending in and getting a floor plan of the building so as to plan a pre-emptive strike.

Weeks passed, and as sure as daylight, Genevieve was honoured for her work. They held a dinner in her name and awarded her the equivalent of a Nobel Peace Prize, recognising her as the mover and shaker she was and her contributions to the community. It was on that evening that she and Dionysus rushed to their car with lust in their minds and intent to rip each other's clothes off as soon as they got home.

As they approached the car, he noticed two SUVs, one parked in front of their car and the other behind it. He presumed it as his paranoia being particularly active, but as he got closer, he spotted a third car parked on the opposite side of the street, making a diamond back formation that they would use to box in their car, a manoeuvre they used in the military. He was about to draw his weapon and initiate a firefight as Genevieve ran for safety but before he could even act, he heard a ballistic bang, a sound he was familiar with, and two seconds later, a projectile pierced his chest! He fell on the ground from the impact as three men exited the vehicles and grabbed Genevieve, putting a dark hood over her head before she could even get to his aid. They dosed her with a sedative and drove off as she slowly lost consciousness.

She could barely gather the strength to open her eyes but her sense of smell was active. She could pick hints of fresh air pouring in from the open car window, indicating that they had left city limits, as Clarence City had a certain industrious scent in the air from factories and overpopulation. She could pick up the smell of cigarettes, Her abductors were smoking. They had a strong infusion of cloves and spice, the tobacco brands only available in Indonesia and North African countries. She took solace in the fact that she could not die at the hands of an enemy and that if her abductors intended to kill her, they would have fired at her and shot her on sight. She came to the conclusion that they were taking her to meet the person who set them loose on her before the sedative they dosed her with took full effect and she passed out for the rest of the journey.

Dionysus got up on his feet and hurriedly made his way to the lobby of the hall the event was taking place in. He fell to the floor as the people present in the room gasped in horror of the sight of his blood-soaked shirt. They ran to his aid, and as luck would have it, there were several doctors in the room. They performed first aid as an ambulance soon came to the premises and took him away to Clarence General hospital.

The doctors rushed in a chaotic fashion, testing and probing, assessing the damage caused by the bullet and prepping him for surgery as he replayed the past events in his head. His heart weighed heavy on him, as he was uncertain of Genevieve's wellbeing. He gathered himself out of a state of distraught and began to think objectively like the skilled soldier he once was.

The fact that he hadn't noticed the diamond back formation of the cars meant that these men were highly trained, that they knew where to find her suggested that they were running surveillance on Genevieve for at least a week, that the bullet that shot him took fairly three seconds before impact meant that they had a sniper over watch and a good one nonetheless. At the standard speed of a bullet, which is twenty-five hundred feet per second, this shot would have travelled an average seventy-five hundred feet, a distance short of two kilometres. If he was using a high-powered rifle, which was safe to assume he was, there were only a few men in the world who could make such a shot. That he chose to shoot from such a distance when he could have easily taken up a closer vantage point signified that the sniper was shooting for sport.

He overheard the men who grabbed her, speaking in an Arabic dialect with some French pronouns, indicating that they were of North African descent. The anaesthesia kicked in and he gave in to its persuasions only after he was certain he had deduced as much of the facts about what had transpired and would have a direction of investigation once he awoke.

Word of her abduction spread like a wildfire and was featured in the news over the weeks. *"FIRST FRUIT CORPORATION CEO AND FOUNDER ABDUCTED!"* the highlights in the papers read somewhere in the article's fine print. They stated that a member of her security detail was gunned down by a presumed sniper. She would have hated the fact that the tabloids defined Dionysus as narrowly as her security detail. Well, in fact he was much more to her.

Jessica assumed Genevieve's roles as per her instructions Should she be on leave or out of commission, she was the one who was probably distraught the most, as she held Genevieve at the highest regard. She had done a lot for her, including mentoring her and taking her under her wing to the point that she could temporarily assume the role of CEO in Clarence City's biggest development firm. She cried and wailed upon news of the misfortune that became upon her and then gathered herself for the work ethic Genevieve instilled in her wouldn't allow her grief to halt productivity, nor would Genevieve approve of her methods if she took a sabbatical out of concern for her.

Mayor Claude was facing pressure from his superiors. The fact that the city's most influential and stand-up citizen had come to harm in her own town of residence was simply unacceptable. The masses demanded answers on investigation progress and the state of her wellbeing. He in turn pressured the local detectives and government investigation apparatus for results. They discovered that the CCTV cameras mounted in the driveway that was the scene of the crime had been tampered with, as they were not functional a few days prior to the incident. They speculated that they were sabotaged by a handheld high-powered military grade laser pointer that ruins camera lenses once they are exposed to the beam. They, however, managed to get the last recorded footage, a well-built man with an apparent burn on his left cheek pointing a peculiar illuminating device at the camera, running facial recognition to no avail. Their only hope was to wait for Dionysus to recover from his medically induced comatose and give his detailed accounts as their saving grace investigation-wise.

She had come to the conclusion that she was out of town. The cold breeze that brushed on her shoulder gave her an incline that she was in an area of high altitude, and based on how long they were on the road, there was only one place that came to mind on where her abductors were keeping her: the Crichton Hills. It was a remote area close to Clarence City that had private estates and ranches. She could hear dogs viciously barking and men who she assumed were their trainers, commanding them in German, *"SITZEN! ATTACKE! KOMME HER!"* It meant, "Sit! Attack! Come here!"

She speculated she was in a militia training ground when she heard gunshots fired frequently and casually with no cause for alarm as they would in a shooting range, and based on how the gunshots sounded like they came from all directions suggested that they had a target-acquisition program with infiltration simulations. It was also the fact that military dogs are typically trained in German so that insurgents do not give them commands in English, which ideally would be their first course of action once the hounds would be unleashed on them. She was truly brilliant. Even while blindfolded and deprived of one of the most crucial senses, she had confidently deduced that her captures were of North African descent, that they were keeping her in a large facility somewhere in the Crichton Hills, and that they had a canine unite and live fire weapon training, so escape would be ill-advised.

A week had passed and she didn't have the slightest clue on who her abductors really were, nor their motives for kidnapping her. They fed her and gave her water, all while blindfolded and bound. They seemed to be extremely cautious of her, suggesting that they knew far more than most people, as there was no cause to perceive an attractive damsel in distress like herself as a threat, unless they knew what she was truly capable of. She found the notion unsettling and began to push for an audience with whoever was in charge. "All in good time, my dear," a man with a deep Tunisian accent said, putting her demands at ease by hinting that the overdue audience was imminent.

She could tell it was past the odd hours of the night, as her internal clock struck 'snooze' and her brain released a dose of melatonin that made her doze off on the chair she was bound in. Her stomach turned when she got abruptly elevated and lifted by her abductors. She took ease at the fact that they were moving her presumably to the audience with their superior that she so desired. After the better part of a hundred paces, they put her down. She could tell that the room they had moved her to was of a different climate. It was temperature-controlled. She assumed also from the acoustics that left her certain that the space was congested and airtight. For the longest time in a long time, she was genuinely scared and concerned for her safety.

"I shall unbind your hands but do not remove your blindfold until I say so," a deep voice instructed her as they cut off her restraints and she heard a buzzing noise as a door slammed behind them and they exited the room, suggesting that the doors were electric, like those of a prison cell. There was no doubt that these men knew exactly who she was and what she had done over the course of history. The fact that they had prepared a facility that could contain her was unsettling and warranting of concern.

"Remove your blindfold," the man who appeared to be giving them orders as a captain to his soldiers gave her the command, to which she complied. Her heart pounded out of her chest when she took out the blindfolds to find herself in a reinforced glass cage in an ill-lit room, though the cage seemed to be running on a different power source. She never realised she was claustrophobic till that particular evening and felt like a caged beast at the zoo. She tried to compose herself to get a read of the room.

They stood around her glass cage, men in suits and men in modern-day warfare attire, armed to the teeth, all standing in ceremoniously around her glass cage at full alert and ready to act should she break loose and turn to the rabid beast they were treating her as.

Her knees wobbled as the men made way for their leader, Fulgar, who walked majestically and with a commanding presence towards her. She hadn't experienced such fear in many a millennia, her face pale in complete terror when she recognised him and even more so as he got closer to the cage. A lot of time had passed but just like she remembered him from her nightmares, there he stood just like the first time she laid eyes on him, surrounded by violently capable men willing to do terrible things on his bidding. Fulgar, meaning lightning in Latin, was a nickname Rome gave to the commander of its most lethal advisory, appropriately named for how rapid his executions of the master strategies he conceived. Before her very eyes stood the man who set her dark path in motion, the same physique and facial symmetry, only this time his pelt and armour were traded in for a three-piece Armani suit. The spears his men wielded traded for carbine rifles. She fell to her knees in absolute despair, for lightning had struck twice and she was once again at the mercy of General Hannibal Barca! Just like her, he hadn't aged a day and appeared to share the same fate of immortality cursed to roam the world's battlefronts over time and millennia war was his food and drink!

Chapter XVIII
Vacuarum Sedium
'Empty Thrones'

Clarence City had witnessed its first period in decades where the largest organizations stood without leadership, leaving a void in some perceived thrones. In the world of organised crime, the era of the Morettis was done and the head of the largest corporation in the city was abducted, leaving authorities stumped and clueless on steps to take in the investigation. Naturally, there would be a few opportunists who would rise to the occasion and attempt to gain control, all in vain! The Irish mob got too bold upon news of the Moretti massacre and attempted to gain turf that they would usually get into a dispute over with their main Italian rivals but the authorities had anticipated a takeover attempt from rival gangs and they set up honey traps that entailed sting operations and undercover entrapment that saw the Irish mob dwindle in ranks as one and all got incarcerated and indicted, embodying the credo, "When it rains, it pours." It was a tough time to be a gangster in the city.

Jessica too wasn't without her woes. Her rise to acting CEO made a lot of the company partners green with envy as some questioned her capability of handling the job and others the justice in her assuming the role, for they had sacrificed more time and effort alike and she was but an errand girl that once served them their morning coffee not too long ago. Their attempt at a hostile corporate takeover was countered accordingly, proving to them that she wasn't just the measly assistant they once knew but a product and ward of the great Genevieve Henrietta.

Genevieve sat in the corner of her cage in a foetal position. She knew what she had witnessed. She just couldn't come to terms and process the events that took place on the night when the man who once caused her so much grief and who she thought was long gone casually walked in the room and turned her whole world upside down. He had walked up to her cage and didn't utter a word. He just stood there staring at her as she came undone, his mouth shut but the grin on his face speaking volumes. He revelled in the moment as she groaned in pain, on her knees, and cursing his existence. Overcome by rage, her omen for the first time was at bay despite of her emotional strain and a rage in her belly that had her in a state of unhinged catalepsy.

He stood for a good while, taking in the view of her in complete anguish. If she was living art in captivity by his hand, she would be his magnum opus. He analysed her pain and movements of frustration from behind the safety of the glass wall. Once he was certain she knew who he was, he left without uttering a single word, planning to return to find a more sober-minded Genevieve or as he remembered her as Giaya, for the unhinged lady who was in front of him was a pale comparison to her, with her head screwed on tight and her wits about herself.

How is that blood thirsty beast still alive? The history books say he took his own life… My omen should have worked! I sold my soul for nothing! A series of questions ran through her mind, leaving more unanswered destructive questions and theories in their wake. She was spiralling and in need of tranquillity and rest. She cried herself to sleep in her corner, her eyes shut, and for the first time since it happened two and a half millennia ago, the lights in her glass cage flickered and flattered as her spirit astro projected back to the dark realm she parted her soul to the mysterious entity in.

She was in a black dress this time as opposed to the white dress she had on the last time she was there. She presumed the colour of her clothing represented purity, white, for when she first appeared to the mysterious place, innocent and impressionable. Now clad I in a dress pitch-black that symbolised what she had become and her misdeeds over time. The ooze was as thick and strange to the touch of the souls of her feet as she remembered. She knew to follow the breeze blowing across her shoulder blades like instinct with hints of *déjà vu*. She walked and pondered and momentarily forgot about her woes that waited for her in reality. A silhouette light brightened a section of absolute black in the direction she was heading in. The man she encountered on her last trip in the rabbit hole stood in front of two massive chairs that would have been adequate thrones for the highest monarchs in any kingdom.

He waited for her to master the courage to approach, and as she did, she noticed the same serpent that bit her right foot so long ago at a spitting distance from where he stood. She dared not forget it. Its menacing girth, length, and overall size still sent a shiver up her spine. Never had she seen its kind since the incident. He was as handsome and youthful as she remembered, his white attire traded in for a modern-day equivalent of a well-tailored suit, his feet just like hers, submerged up to his shins on the gooey substance on the floor. His distinctive scent of burned sage etched in her memory like a photographer's favourite picture. There was a cordial smile on his face. This time, she would be inquisitive and cautious of any arrangements made with this strange entity of a man, for the last bargain they struck turned her into stuff of nightmares.

"Ravishing," he complimented her as she strut closer to her. His voice was like the after-rumble of thunder that would terrify anyone but her, for she had already witnessed his intimidating appearance and that to her humanised him despite his godlike presence.

"I suppose I have you to thank," she casually responded.

"When you first came to me, you were pure, innocent, a victim of war seeking sweet vengeance with a rage burning like the fires of hell. I, however, never explained my motives or intentions, for your feeble human mind couldn't comprehend or fathom my methods or understand my objectively maniacal plan. You have come a long way and have earned an explanation.

"The powers that reign on my side of the spectrum had come to the unanimous decision that we would not meddle in the affairs of man. I was given an exception to create a counter to represent my bidding against my direct opposition, a champion who would be an answer to his light, malice to his benevolence through my will. One chance, one champion, my concealed dagger, my secret weapon to eventually become mankind's undoing. All hope was lost until you called onto me in the shores of the first land. There in front of me stood the perfect subject, a natural beauty. Evil attributes a weapon forged by the cruelty of men. I but only had to give you the means and set you loose on them, the means of which you would only come by if you parted with your soul." Her heart pounded in horror as he explained his dark motives.

"You would wield the power of sexual lust, every man's weakness, and your persuasions would be undeniable. The first recipient of your wrath would share your fate and become your lifetime partner, strongest ally in the battle against light. He would wield the power of war and cause good grief upon the world." She trembled in terror when he explained her presumed role in the world, confirming her suspicions that she was in the presence of the pure evil that all earthly religions depict. "In the spirit of acting against my direct opposite, I decided to do things completely as such… opposite. Up would be down, in, out, and the cross inverted! He made man first. I made woman. He made woman out of man's ribs. I made a man from your wrath, the first recipient of your abilities, the man who set your path in my direction and currently has you in captivity… my champion of war!

"You as my chosen shall explain his role to him and continue doing my bidding with a sense of purpose and direction. He has not earned an audience with me and would most likely turn unhinged upon my presence. Upon fulfilment of my will and the world turns to a pile of ash and debris, you shall join me on my right-hand side. Only then will we sit on these empty thrones in front of us with my pet, Beilzedad, at our feet, for now they remain as vacuarium sedium." The snake that he deemed as his pet hissed loudly as she snapped back to the realm of reality, waking up, her feet peculiarly covered in dark ooze, hyperventilating and terrified.

Chapter XIX
Wine and Dinner

Dionysus came to. He was disoriented at first. The medically induced coma the doctors put him in to reduce inflammation had taken a lot from him. He was slightly sore but there was minimal tissue damage from the bullet. The sniper was aiming for his heart and missed by a feather probably from Dionysus's sudden movements upon realising he was walking into an ambush. He tried to gather his thoughts and recollection of past events as his train of thoughts prior to being incapacitated started to flood back in.

He ran a recap in his mind, a group of men that moved as a unit and communicated in an Arabic and French dialect, suggesting that they were of North African descent. They executed a diamond back formation manoeuvre so discreetly that even a seasoned soldier as himself couldn't see it until it was too late. They also had an extremely talented sniper over watch that could make a shot from a disturbingly long distance. These were not ordinary men; they were highly trained professionals, either active or former military, and since he could not think of any foreign government factions that would want to abduct Genevieve, he came to the conclusion that they were private security.

In his time as a soldier in Afghanistan when Nathan was still alive, his commanding officer had sent them to infiltrate a compound full of insurgents. As the senate had not deployed the necessary manpower, they were to work with some contractors that apparently had a very high mission-success rate. The name of the company eluded him momentarily, as he was still gathering his strength and reasoning but he recalled that it was based in Tunisia and that they were the top-pick contractors for most western countries with troops in the Middle East.

Among their ranks was the only sniper who was arguably just as good a shot as him if not better. He had a chance to get acquainted. He was well built, a close quarter's combat master and even more lethal from a mile out with a high-powered rifle. An incident occurred on that mission where an improvised explosive device went off meters away from his vantage point, injuring the mysterious presumed sniper and leaving him with a nasty napalm burn on his left cheek. He was almost certain that he had found the perpetrators of her abduction. However, their motive was still unclear. They gave their services to the highest bidder and only worked in battlefields and warfronts.

If they were under an individual's employment, he or she would have had to part with a pretty penny, more than the trouble's worth. It began to dawn on him that her abduction was personal. Someone was settling a score. He remembered how he once met the CEO and founder of the security group after they completed the mission. He congratulated them on a job well done and tried to recruit him in his ranks, of which he declined, for men like him and his went to war for the thrill of the fight and glory of battle, not for honour.

'Fulgar! Of Fulgar Security Solutions.' Dionysus overcame his tip-of-the-tongue syndrome as the founder and private security company's name came to him.

Mayor Claude walked in his ward with a companion as well as his assigned physician. "The mayor and his companion would like to ask you some investigation-related questions," the physician asked, as it was due processes to announce to the patient the presence of guests and their purpose of visit. "Would you like to host them now or would you prefer them to come later?" Dionysus gave the physician a nod of approval as he signalled them in.

"Mr. Dionysus, good to see you awake. I hope you are recovering well."

"I… I'm, sir," he responded, his sense of decorum still active from his military days.

"I believe you are acquainted with Agent Brown," the mayor continued. Upon paying close attention, he realised the mayor's companion was none other than Archer Brown. They worked in the same unit and he was his brother at arms for an entire tour. He had left the military and was now a federal agent.

"Over watch, only you can turn priesthood into a dangerous profession." They all chuckled at Brown's witty salutation of sorts.

"I see your sense of humour is still as terrible as I remember," Dionysus responded, adding laughter to the playful mood of the room and spark to the reunion.

"As much as I wish this were a social visit, we have some pressing issues to address," the mayor said, shifting the direction of the banter to a more serious nature.

"Agent Brown is in charge of the unit tasked to finding your employer and friend, Genevieve Henrietta. We have stumbled upon a hurdle in our investigation and we were hoping you could help with your witness accounts, as you were the last person to see her before her abduction. I came to formally introduce both of you in a professional capacity as well as wishing you a speedy recovery. Now that that's done, I shall make my leave and let you gentlemen discuss." He shook Dionysus's hand and exited the room.

"Piece of work. That fellow, he didn't even bring you get-well-soon flowers and a fresh pair of diapers." Dionysus laughed hysterically at Archer's inappropriate joke at the highest-ranking government official's cost.

"Can't tell you how good it is to see you, Arch."

"Likewise," Archer responded. "So what can you tell me of the night you got shot?" he continued, getting straight to the heart of the matter.

Dionysus took a moment to respond as he weighed his options on whether to inform him of his theory that was probably accurate or to wait until he could get back on his feet and rescue her with a hail of bullets paired with retribution of a biblical proportion. He came to the conclusion that his recovery would take the better part of the week and that he needed assistance from the authorities, since they had more resources and were just as motivated to find her as he was, it was bad press that the most valued citizen had been abducted in her own city and investigators were stumped.

"I obviously can't tell you all the excruciating details but I'll tell you what transpired and my working theory on one condition."

"What is it?" he asked, eager to gather the intelligence he was holding out on.

"The condition is that you include me in the investigation as a consultant and that you let me ride in when the raid takes place."

"I'll check with my superiors but that shouldn't be an issue. You have combat training and are quite possibly pound for pound the best shot in the country."

"I'm obviously not a priest anymore."

"Obviously!" Agent brown added. They both smiled and chuckled, taking a brief moment to suppress their laughter before Dionysus continued telling his accounts as an investigative statement.

"I work as Genevieve Henrietta's bodyguard, an all-round right-hand man. It's not known to the public but she and I are involved and have been seeing each other after hours. She had no immediate enemies that she could name, so a security detail was available to her but not necessarily, a notion I wish I was less in the perception of, for it made me drop my guard and fail to pick up on the tells of surveillance her abductors presumably ran days, even weeks, prior to the attack.

"We were leaving the gala dinner where she got awarded and recognised for her contributions to the community and her company's achievements of infrastructure. The mood was festive and we were rushing back to her place to celebrate privately and intimately while in the driveway making our way to the vehicle. There were two cars parked, one ahead of her town car and the other behind it. I thought nothing of it until we got closer and I noticed a third car parked on the other side of the street directly opposite to where we were. It then dawned on me that they were priming for a diamond back manoeuvre, so I reached for my gun to initiate suppressing fire as she escaped but before I could draw my weapon, I heard a ballistic blast echoing from a distance and three seconds later, I winced in pain as a bullet pierced my chest.

"I fell to the ground but before I was temporarily incapacitated, I saw three men in black suits exit the vehicles and grab her, putting a hood over her head. They communicated in a dialect mixed with French and Arabic. They made a hasty exit and I passed out momentarily, only to awake and find my way to the hall where I was assisted accordingly.

"These are the facts and actual events of what transpired. My working theory is another thing entirely. Would you care to hear it?"

"Please!" Archer Brown responded, his curiosity fully peaked.

"They pulled off surveillance and a diamondback maneuver flawlessly to the extent that a seasoned and adequately trained professional as myself was oblivious to what was happening until it was too late, suggesting that they were not the typical criminals but had a military background. They spoke in an Arabic and French dialect, indicating that they were of North African descent. They had a clear exit strategy that signified that they were very good at their job, and finally the sniper over watch, he shot me from an estimated distance of no less than two kilometres. He could have easily have gotten a closer vantage point but he chose to do it from a record-breaking distance either to challenge himself or for the sake of sport. Only a handful of men could have executed that shot and hit their target from that distance. You should know... I'm one of them.

"I can give an educated guess that they were paramilitary and of North African descent, very efficient, and particularly skilled with an extremely talented sharpshooter in their ranks. The peculiarity of the evidence brought me back to my military days. One operation in particular where my unit had to procure the services of a contractor due to lack of manpower, not just any contractor but the best in the business with a sharpshooter in their ranks that could give me a run for my money. During the operation an improvised explosive device went off close to his vantage point, a Noremco Industries' warhead that was opened and filled with c4 plastic explosives and hidden unassumingly in a pile of garbage, leaving the sniper with a visible third-degree burn on his left cheek." He paused to catch his breath and continued, "We completed the objective and their CEO and founder met us at the base with our commanding officer to congratulate us. He discreetly tried to recruit me but I turned down his offer. His name was Mr. Fulgar of..."

"... FULGAR SECURITY SOLUTIONS!" They said it in unison as Agent Archer marvelled at his exceptional deductive and reasoning skills, for he too had heard of FSS, a Tunisian-based paramilitary group that was on the beck and call of most global military juggernauts as contractors for their unique skills and success rate.

Agent Archer Brown's doubts shifted to certainty when he recalled the last recorded footage he got from the scene of the abduction of a well-built man pointing a handheld military-grade laser that tampered with the camera lenses and how he did not show up in any databases, collaborating

Dionysus's theory of the sniper in Fulgar's employment with a noticeable burn on his left cheek. Agent Archer Brown's investigation finally had a direction, thanks to Dionysus's input. He knew who the perpetrators were. He just couldn't reconcile their motives as to why they would want to abduct Genevieve Henrietta. Financial motivations were out of the question as they were the highest grossing paramilitary faction in the world and had more resources than a third-world nation army, including a fleet of MIG thirty-five jets, predator drones, tanks, and a submarine that could fire intercontinental ballistic missiles.

Dionysus coughed and whizzed violently, disrupting Archer's train of thoughts and replacing them with genuine concern as he reached to his aid with a glass of water that was on his bed stand. "You should get some much-needed rest. Let me look into your theory, which will most probably pan out. I'll use my military connections to find out if there were any sanctioned missions within city limits. If not, then that means Mr. Fulgar and his men are acting in their own accord and that warrants some concern for national security." Dionysus took a sip of his water and cleared his throat.

"I suggest you look into shell corporations under Fulgar Security Solutions. See if they have any properties listed or have procured any within the last six months, estates or ranches in the outskirts of town, someplace big enough for them to train. I could wager that they are keeping her in such a place. I'll rest and recover and then come to you. Hopefully you will have discovered their location by then." Agent Brown bid him farewell as Dionysus closed his eyes to rest and with the objective to fully recover from his injuries. Genevieve had now grown accustomed to her new environment that was the glass cage with the essentials to keep a person in captivity for a long period of time, a toilet seat on the far corner of the cage, a sink, a bar of soap and towels close by a bed covered in thin sheets not of the thousand thread-count variety she would prefer but she made due, her state of mind a far cry from that of fear and distraught that they brought her in. She was back to her calm, confident, ace-up-my-sleeve demeanour, no doubt a result of the audience with the dark entity who explained the purpose of all that was happening and her cataclysmic role in the future, of which she intended to oppose with every fiber of her being.

Fulgar was monitoring her from a tablet screen that was always in his possession as it was linked to the cameras in the glass cage. He enjoyed watching her come undone and pace around in frustration when she was brought in for the first time and he watched in terror as the lights flickered and faltered moments before her spirit astro projected as he hastily ordered Cassim to stand watch outside the cage, bearing first-hand witness of what was transpiring.

He marvelled in disbelief as sparks and ashy debris filled the air, a sight that was blind to the naked eye based on Cassim's accounts but clearly visible through the footage, a distorted image of a ridiculously tall and built man in the modern-day equivalent of a well-tailored white suit again visible on camera, but based on Cassim's take on the matter, there was no one but Genevieve in the room. According to the timeframe that all of these events unfolded, the climate-controlled room that was set to a moderate and reasonable temperature had mysteriously dropped to a crisp, chilly, and brutal −6.66 Celsius for an hour!

Fulgar jerked back from his seat in horror when he saw her awake from her trance and pace around in confusion and adrenaline leaving behind dark oily footprints on the floor as she walked, her feet covered in dark ooze that was mysteriously not on her prior to the terrifying phenomenon.

Paradoxically less there was a tub of crude oil, of which she soaked her feet in her confinement, of which there was none. She hadn't moved an inch after the lights began to flicker either. He would give himself and her time to overcome their fear and gather their wits before giving her the audience. She deserved a conversation over a heavily guarded wine and dining experience.

Cassim walked over to her glass confinement after things had settled down and she was as nonchalant as anyone could possibly be in her situation. He had a white box in hand. She was familiar with the packaging, as she left with a similar box of exact width and length every time she went shopping for a dress. For the first time since they put her there, he opened the magnetised door. She stepped back as he made his way in and placed the box on the bed.

"For tonight," he said as he walked away. The notion of escape was moronic. Even if she managed to incapacitate a man of his size, the compound was heavily guarded and monitored. The only way she was leaving was if she was rescued or if Barca let her go. Besides, she was curious about what the proper audience with Barca would entail. She presumed it would feature a quick sum down on what happened to him after she used her omen on him. She opened the box and as certain as daylight, in it was a black dress that would undoubtedly complement her figure and expose an absurd amount of skin based on the slits of its hinges and backless design. She smiled not at the gesture but at the inappropriateness of it all, something she had come to expect from Barca.

Dionysus had regained motor skills from his right side and his stitches had begun to hold as the surgical strings merged with his skin. He was out of the woods and only felt a sharp pain when he made sudden movements. He was checked out of the hospital and was prescribed a strong dosage of painkillers that numbed all the pain a person recovering from a gunshot wound would have experienced. His first order of business was to get in touch with Agent Archer Brown to check on his progress. He promised him that he was onto something, sparing the details for a face-to-face meeting that he scheduled for the next day, as the line was not encrypted and their adversaries were capable men that could easily infiltrate and listen in on telecommunications on most if not all secure networks.

He had the evening to himself to settle back into his day-to-day life. He made his way to Genevieve's townhouse as they were cohabiting. The elevator doors opened and at the back of his mind, he was hoping she would be there to receive him in sexy lingerie and a glass of bourbon in hand like she once did but owe unto him! The harsh reality was slowly setting in when he walked into a dark living room.

He used the module hub on the wall to turn on the lights. The place was just as he left it, a banner on the wall that read congratulations, rose petals and confetti on the floor, and champagne on a bucket half full with room-temperature water that was once ice. He had taken the liberty of having the place made to look festive in order to surprise her after the gala. He picked up a pillow that she liked to lie her head on whenever they lay on the couch, smothering his face with it and inhaling. Oh, how it carried her scent! Tears fell from his eyes freely as he dropped to his knees and let out a scream in emotional anguish, his face plunged into the pillow that muffled his screams of distraught. This was the first time he let himself have the appropriate reaction to what had happened. He could not stay at a place that carried so many memories of her. The fact that there was so much comfort and luxury around him and he wasn't even sure if she had a roof over her head or a coat to keep her warm ate at him like a predator would devour prey. He made a quick exit, turning off the lights on the hub before getting into the elevator, setting course to his storage unit at the docks that would have passed for an arsenal. He would spend the evening cleaning, polishing, lubricating, and aligning his collection of firearms, as he found it therapeutic and purpose-relevant, the purpose being preparing for war!

She put on the dress provided and tied her hair into a bun, exposing her long feminine neck and earlobes. She didn't have her usual tools of seduction like pearls and perfume but she knew her audience and had it on good authority that Barca had an erotic asphyxiation and found a woman's neck to be the most sensual part of her anatomy, information she came about as his concubine millennia ago that somehow remained etched in memory.

She was famished and eagerly waited to be summoned, entertaining an incline that there would be a spread of some sort, for he wouldn't parade her in such a dress simply for his viewing pleasure. The clock struck 8 p.m. and Cassim appeared like a fairy, a fairy with a nasty burn on his left cheek and a sand-gripped Glock Seventeen visible on his unbuttoned holster and probably loaded with a bullet in the chamber for quick and lethal force if necessary. The magnetised door buzzed before he flung it open and entered. He gaped at her *attrait sexuel* before collecting his thoughts and carrying out Fulgar's instructions to guide her to the dining area. "Follow!" he commanded and she obliged, walking a few paces behind him and getting familiar with her surroundings that she hadn't seen, since she was brought into her confinement blindfolded.

They walked past a long corridor with ten doors, five on each side, left and right. She managed to catch a glimpse through one of the doors that was not fully closed, exposing living quarters with two beds on each side of the wall. On the terrible excuse for a table was a rifle, a bottle of vodka, and a half-smoked cigarette on the ashtray that made the entire corridor smell like spice and cloves. She tried to get a closer look but a shirtless, hairy man walked to the door and shut it, no doubt one of the occupants of the room reminding her to mind her wandering eyes. She could safely assume that the other rooms had a similar layout and the same number of occupants, making the place a fortress, seeing as how there were ten rooms with two occupants per room, adding up to at least twenty agitators in the compound if basic mathematics is anything to go by.

He guided her past the garden and water feature that had a marble-curved statue embodying the essence of Barca. "I see his vanity has remained intact over the years," she said as he looked back at her and contained his immediate instinct to smile at her witty remark.

"Keep up!" He used a harsh tone to establish his dominance and enforce her captive's psychosis, for she seemed oddly comfortable at the mercy of her captures. Her level of acceptance to what was happening was vexing to him. They walked past the kennel where the dogs barked viciously, making her heart race. Belgium Melanious were a viscous, energetic breed. They barked, sending a shiver down her spine and chasing away whatever modicum of hope or fantasy of escape she entertained as the second pea in the pod. Even if she managed to elude the presumed twenty highly trained and heavily armed personnel in the premises, the hounds would catch up to her.

They had made their way to the main house where a grand crystal chandelier hung from the ceiling. The floor was Italian marble, the furniture of white leather, and specific areas of the floor carpeted in animal hide, reminding her of the saying "Old habits die hard," for he was a hide collector when she first met him.

Men armed with rifles, guarding exits and corridors. *He must have a lot of enemies,* she thought to herself as his pace slowed to match hers, indicating that they were close to their destination. She could smell seared onions and garlic, confirming her suspicions that she would be joining him for dinner. She was craving fish. A nice grilled salmon or steamed sea bass would have satisfied her. They were soon at the dining area. He had options of tables they could have occupied, the smaller ones where they could have sat side by side as they talked. Instead, he opted for the long rectangular table where they sat at opposite heads. On the spread fit for a king were chunks of grilled salmon, a well-crafted and put-together salad plate, and strip loin. She came to the conclusion that the food on the table was either a display of extravagance or more likely the soldiers would have at it once they were done with their session.

"Breathtaking!" he complimented her as she gave him a spin to admire what he once owned.

"The dress you picked for me fits like a glove, a bold move. I would expect nothing less," she responded to Fulgar's complement as Cassim pulled the chair back and she sat. "The only issue is that you are sitting soo far away." She had put aside any resentment she had for him, for just like her, he was immortal and could keep her as his captive for eternity if he willed it.

"Let's not be unnecessarily cordial. I took everything from you and broke your heart to a million pieces when I had your family and kin slaughtered before your very eyes. Let's not pretend that you wouldn't slit my throat at the first chance you got." She laughed at the accuracy of the comment. He joined her in laughter, though there was nothing comical about the banter.

One of his men traded his rifle for a bottle of wine. He presented the bottle to her just as to inform her on what she was about to consume. The label read: *'Chateauneuf-du-pape.'* She was familiar with the bottle from her time in France in the Second World War. *'Chateauneuf-du-pape'* literally translates to 'new castle of the pope,' taking its name from the time when the pope moved to Avignon in the early 1300s due to conflict between the king of France and the papacy. The grape was grown from vines in the estate. "Interesting choice of wine. Are you serving it coincidentally or are you about to reveal your demented version of poetic justice?" He laughed at the accuracy of her intuition as she sipped the ruby-red wine, savouring the vintage, appreciating the scent of red fruit and oak on the nose, the taste of toast berries and vanilla on the palette and the finish that was high in tannin, leaving her mouth dry and ready to dine.

"I thought the wine was appropriate, seeing how you are now going by the name of Genevieve, the patron saint of Paris who was said to have saved the city by diverting Attila's Huns by prayer, a lady who dedicated herself to Christianity. Her attribute is a candle, and she is sometimes also depicted with the devil, who is said to have blown it out when she went to pray in church at night. Curious choice in identity indeed, though I wonder why you decide to assume the alter ego? Is it because you see yourself as the good saint that dedicated her life to Christianity? Or the devil that blows out the candle when she goes to pray in church at night?" His intelligence matched hers, and for the first time, she was completely clueless on what he would say or do next. "Hence the wine. It features Christianity and conflict. Salute!" He raised his glass and took a gulp all in one sip like the brut he was, some of the precious elixir spilling down his chin and cheeks onto the table.

The grilled salmon was calling to her like a siren cry. She stuck her fork into the fleshy steak and placed it on her plate, cutting off a huge chunk and consuming it. "I was famished," she said as soon as she swallowed. "You threw a stab at the dark and hit a target. I chose the name Genevieve because of her unique perceived conflict. I must admit your reasoning skills are nothing short of impressive. It's no wonder that all high-ranking generals and military personnel study your war strategies. Your abstract thinking earned you a spot in the history books. They even named a city in Spain after you. Barcelona derived from the word 'Barca.' Obviously I've never been there because I hated you with every fiber of my being. I still do but I guess time heals all wounds to a certain degree. What happened to you after the Punic War? I assume the history books are all hogwash when it comes to your story."

"Well, for some unknown reason, since I last saw your true face, I opted to go over the Alps with my entire fleet." She picked up on his sarcasm. "If you know your history, then you know that it took a great toll on my dwindling ranks that had to fight the harsh weather elements, not to mention vicious indigenous Roman tribes. I was out of sorts and was acting unlike my usual self, for if I was of sound mind, I never would have attempted to go over the treacherous mountains. I would have gone around them and would have overcome the Roman Army as a result. Could you imagine the implications my victory would have had in the world? Carthage would have been the hub of civilization. Roman democracy that is still used today by the world's super power countries would be a thing of the past. Christianity would not be legitimised. Greece would not exist and South Africa would be a Phoenician state. Greatness! Glory! That's what you took from me, witch!"

She jerked back at her seat from his sudden outrage. "The price for immortality, I guess," she responded to his insult before he continued telling his story. "What the history books fail to mention is that I fell in battle just as I was about to sack Rome. One of the soldiers drove his gladius clean through my chest and I was dead before I hit the ground. They say that I returned to defend Carthage, leaving Rome ripe for the plucking but I assure you that was not the case. I had asked the men to abandon the campaign and take me home should I fall in battle." He opened his shirt, exposing the scar from the stab. "As I lay on the horse carriage dead, I had a dream that I was in a room with dark ooze fairly three inches thick on the floor, a place not of this world, and I heard a voice rumble like thunder, saying, 'It is done!' Next thing I know, I wake up gasping for air to find my wound healed and a room full of moaners standing where I lay in utter shock that I had conquered death.

"Rome had gained momentum, advancing towards the heart of Carthage and a bargain had to be struck to save the city. I ended up in modern-day Turkey and then Greece, where my agelessness was beginning to show, so as a fugazee and to stop an all-out bounty for my head, I drank poison in front of witnesses who pronounced me dead, only to arise again. I assumed the nickname they had given me, Fulgar, as a memento of my hay days and I have been raging terrible war in this blue globe we call Earth since then, shifting the course of battles, rewriting history and handing power to empires, kings, and presidents, wielding weapons from short swords to knight's amour to muskets to automatic weapons and nuclear bombs."

"Your purpose of existence seems crystal-clear. I can't help but wonder why you sort me out and how you tied me to your phenomenal lifespan." She bit off another chunk of salmon and chewed, taking advantage of the fact that it was Fulgar's turn to talk.

"Well, I had a lot of time to think and come up with theories and hypothesis that best supported my predicament. At first, I thought myself special and chosen by God but as the secrets of science got revealed to man over time, I doubted my reasoning, putting my pride aside. I broke down the facts of my last encounter with you before falling in battle for the first time. I remember walking into your chambers with lustful intentions, your eyes changing into a terrible serpent-like yellow when I was on top of you, and the next thing I remember was that I had this insatiable urge to set you free from the role of concubine and changing the trajectory of my march to take on the Alps with my entire fleet! Thus, the beginning of my ruination naturally I spent most of my existence searching for you, unsure whether you shared my fate as an immortal or caused it. It wasn't until recently that I got the unshakable feeling, a hunch if you will, that I would find you in Clarence City.

"I brought the best men in my ranks and began to search for you, block by block, turf by turf. We were about to lose all hope and pack our bags, leaving for the Middle East when Cassim walked in my office with information that he had seen a lady matching your description on the television. I turned on my TV set, and as certain as death, there you were, as young and beautiful as I remembered. I had no doubt that you were responsible for my current state. In fact, I began to suspect that you shared my fate.

"So I began running surveillance on you to see what type of person time had turned you into, for you were a far cry from my sweet, innocent Giaya. The most enjoyable sight was watching you achieve greatness, rebuilding an entire city skyline with your designs. Even I can admit that was a great feat.

"I knew I had the element of surprise, so I set my men loose on you when you were leaving the gala, events unfolding to this very moment with a *chateauneuf-du-pape* serving as social lubricant… Meticulous!"

She took a sip of wine and cleared her throat and added, "Now that we are done exchanging speculations and educated guesses, let's talk facts and queries. Mine which I'm sure you have figured out by now is why you have me locked up in the equivalent of a dry human-sized aquarium. Yours I can presume but I would like to hear it come from your tongue in the off-chance that my logic is incorrect."

"Enough with the games!" he shouted in anger, knocking down the dining paraphernalia on his side of the table, the bottle of wine unfortunately being one of them, an expensive tantrum, she thought as he belched out his frustrations, "What are you? Why can't we die!" The guards moved closer to the table, alert for signs of a rising altercation.

"I wouldn't pretend to give you instructions, but I recommend that you sit down for this, for I'm about to unravel the mysteries that eat at you, shaking you to your core while doing so." He sat and remained quiet, eager to hear her accounts.

"It all started after you raided my village and your men tied me up to a tree to bear witness to the horrible pillage and plunder. Just like you, I spent years in research and archaeology, searching for an explanation for why the dark entity chose me to be his champion. Turns out that my village was on the shores of the four intersecting rivers that were slowly submerging the island in their intersection, leaving only a great oak at its peak that appeared to be floating on water as an optical illusion. He called it the first land. If you know or practice theology, you would know that the submerging island was the one and only Garden of Eden, the tree being the tree of life, so your war crimes happening at such a peculiar location by definition sealed our fate and, as I have recently discovered, intertwined them, eventually leading to a world on fire and a glassily cataclysmic grand finale that you and I would be the root cause of.

"I… I closed my eyes in hopes of never opening them again when my spirit astro projected to the realm of absolute darkness with a dark ooze on the floor fairly three inches thick. I believe it to be the same place you went when you died. However, you spent but a brief moment and didn't make the acquaintance of the inhabitant of the terrifying realm… I spent the entire evening!" His heart raced and his hands trembled. Never had he known true horror even when he faced certain death. "I walked to him and he received me. He offered me the means to exact vengeance on you and your men at the price of my soul. Upon accepting his terms, strange things happened. Then you came to claim me as your spoils of war under the tree your men had bound me in." She left out the crucial details of the serpent and her infinity-symbol tattoo.

"It wasn't until you tried to practice your sexual deviance on me that I came by my gift, the ability to sway all men who lust for me to do my bidding. You must understand that I hated you with a passion of Biblical proportion but I had to be crafty on how I was going to take my vengeance as you lay there in a trance, susceptible to my will. I thought of having taken your own life but your men would never believe that you were that weak-willed and would immediately presume me as the perpetrator. That's when I came across your war table and it dawned on me that if I set your campaign out on course to take on the Alps, it would mean certain demise for you and your men.

"That however was a very long time ago. Let's talk about more recent transgressions. I'm certain that you are having me watched in my enclosure and probably bore witness, first-hand or otherwise, to the horrific events that took place in my human 'aquarium' a few nights ago," she said sarcastically and continued, "The same phenomenon responsible for our inhumanly long existence took place in your very own home, or should I say fortress?" She gave him a cheeky look that gave him the impression that she wasn't oblivious as he thought her to be. "He summoned me once more after two millennia to explain his motives behind our creation!" His eyes widened in disbelief, curiosity at its highest peak, an emotion that could only be matched by the terror her tale brought. She took a sip of what was left of her wine and Fulgar signalled one of his men to refill her glass, as he had another bottle of the same brand and vintage on standby. He figured the seamless flow of wine would enable her storytelling serving as a mild truth serum if the old quote of Gaius Plinius the elder, *"In vino varitus,"* was anything to go by.

"He is the prince of darkness!"

"I was his first creation, an equivalent to Adam and you, my Eve!" He got winded and exhaled deeply. His stomach turned and had he not have been sitting down, his wobbly knees would not support his weight. "Just as my tool of destruction is lust, yours is war. We are his champions and together as allies, we are supposed to bring about a cataclysm that brings mankind to its knees, leaving behind scorched earth as we join him in the realm of nothingness to claim our *vacuarum sedium* his pet, Beilzedad, at our feet and him at our side." He went pale and silent as she took a huge gulp of her wine.

He was going to get sick and needed some air. He hastily left the dining area and stepped out to the porch as the men read the room and approached her to take her back to her enclosure. She finished the last gulp of her wine and obliged to Cassim's command to stand and walk, and she lay on her bed in her glass cage satisfied with how the night turned out. She whispered beneath her breath, "Nothing beats a dark reckoning over wine and dinner."

Chapter XX
"Deus Ex Machina"
God from a Machine

Agent Archer Brown and his taskforce had located the compound which Fulgar and his men had occupied, thanks to Dionysus's help. The government entity that had granted them access into the country had not given them the authority to bear arms or run a military operation during their stay. Therefore, by doing so, they lost all diplomatic immunity rights and were subject to prosecution, giving Agent Archer Brown and his men jurisdiction to breach the compound and exchange fire if fired upon.

Arial footage of the compound showed multiple agitators and several canines, also a live simulation training ground and what they assumed was an inbuilt shooting range, suggesting that they were armed to the teeth. The reputation that followed them gave them an incline that breaching the compound would not be an easy task, for they were known to have some of the best operators in the world. Fulgar spared no expense when it came to recruiting. He believed in specialised work as opposed to the jack-of-all-trades approach most military factions take. He would add to his ranks the best snipers, explosive experts, war medics, battle infantry, and weapons experts, having them stick to the roles of their trade. That way, he would have the best man for the job when any of their expertise were required.

Dionysus's injuries had healed but he was in no condition to wield his usual long-range, high-powered rifle or anything that had too much of a kickback. He was to meet Archer and his team at first light at a safehouse about two kilometres away from the compound. They were going to breach the fortress by sunrise. He prepared his tools of battle, grabbing a Karambit, which is a small Indonesian knife resembling a claw that most special forces soldiers favour over the straight black blade for its agility and inconspicuous design; he hardly got to use it as no enemy ever survived his drawn fire arm.

He then grabbed a pistol that he used as his secondary weapon, a sand-gripped Glock forty-five with an extended magazine, a compressor at the muzzle tip to expel gases upwards, fighting the recoil whenever fired and a lightweight trigger that increased its rate of fire, taking five magazines and leaving for the rendezvous clad in a black suit. He was going to get her back even if it meant that he would die in the attempt.

The men were geared for the battle in bulletproof vests, helmets, breaching devices, and enough firepower to take on an army. Seeing as how Fulgar and his men had hounds in the compound, Archer Brown mandated that there be no service dogs involved in the operation, as their dogs were trained to only attack human assailants and would surely be in harm's way should they face off with Fulgar's hounds.

"Welcome to the party, Dionysus," Archer greeted his old brother at arms as they were about to begin a briefing on how the breach would be carried out. "Gather around, gentlemen," he summoned the group of heavily armed men to lay out a final action plan. They soon stood in front of him at attention, eager to hear what he had to say.

"The compound we are about to breach is occupied by highly trained and heavily armed assailants. Satellite imaging suggests that they have dogs and possibly an underground facility. Our target is their hostage, Genevieve Henrietta, who was abducted and we believe is being held captive in the premises. We shall heed to the rules of engagement where by the vehicle's mounted PA loud speaker system, we shall announce to them that we are about to breach the compound, giving them a thirty-minute window to surrender and lay down their arms.

"We shall then breach the compound with zero resistance, searching it from hook, line, and sinker until we find our target and apprehend every living occupant in the area. However, if we encounter resistance, we are authorised to use deadly force. Are we clear?" he asked.

"YES, SIR!" they responded in unison as they got into their black armoured vehicles that would have passed for tanks had they mounted canons. Dionysus was hot on their trail in his motorcycle until they came to a stop at the main gate of the compound.

"FEDERAL AGENTS, WE HAVE A WARRANT TO SEARCH THE COMPOUND. DO NOT RESIST. LAY DOWN YOUR ARMS AND PREPARE TO BE BREACHED!"

Archer repeated several times on the vehicle's loud speaker PA system as they waited restlessly for the thirty minute window to close. Dionysus was hoping for a fight. He fantasised emptying his gun on the sniper that nearly took his life. The men got into position as the armoured car reversed so as to gain momentum to run down the gate as the men came rushing in weapons hot should they encounter resistance.

"SIR!" Cassim came barging in Fulgar's office.

"Remind me to train you on how to knock," he responded patronisingly for his lack of decency.

"I apologise, sir, but we have federal agents outside with a breach team announcing that they have a warrant to search the compound. I figure we have thirty minutes or less to lay down our arms and surrender or to prepare for a gunfight. The men are ready to do both. What would you like us to do?"

"Initiate 'God fall,'" he said ominously.

"Are you certain, sir?" Cassim asked and was met with a harsh look that instantly reminded him of his place and who he was addressing.

"I'll be with our guest; come for me when it's done." He used a calm tone but there was no mistaking his request for anything short of an order.

"Consider it done, sir!" he said as he left with purpose.

Genevieve had picked up on the fact that something was going on in the compound. The men were arming themselves and moving about in an unusually fast pace. They appeared to be vacating the place as they moved with luggage and the hounds through a mysterious exit. She speculated that the place was getting attacked but wouldn't get her hopes up until her suspicions were confirmed. Fulgar had made his way to her enclosure. He knocked on the glass window to announce his presence. She was startled. "What's going on?" she asked.

"It would appear the authorities have discovered your location." She smiled at his perceived woes only to remember who she was addressing. Then her smile faded, for he was 'the' soldier and the war champion of the dark entity. Whoever challenged him in battle would face certain death. Even prior to his immortality, he was a formidable warrior.

"Don't hurt them!" she pleaded with him as she remembered what he was capable of, and the fact that the authorities had found where she was being held captive meant that Dionysus assisted them with their investigation and was probably part of the raid. He would have met his doom fighting against him. She couldn't fathom losing everything to the same man twice.

"I have a proposition for you. Come with me." She looked back at him, surprised by his outrageous request as he began to rationalise his madness.

"Thanks to you, I now know my purpose. Wars end. Wars begin, and as much as I enjoy battle, I have always entertained the idea of a grander purpose behind all the kingdoms I have sacked and the lives I have taken. Thanks to you, I now know the cause of my existence. Whether you intend on fulfilling the dark entity's plans or opposing them, there is no denying that we can't do either on our lonesome, only as a unit. Besides, there's still a lot to learn of our unique dynamic and collective predicament, and if we part ways now, it could be centuries, even millennia, until we see each other again, seeing as how we both have a flair for elusiveness. Come with me. Let's discover our predicament together and decide whether we will play the roles given to us or oppose them."

His madness was contagious and she saw the reason behind his argument. She was also keen on getting Dionysus out of his path. "On two conditions." She broke her silence to state her terms of agreement.

"Name it," he responded.

"I will no longer be your captive but honoured guest with freedom of movement and access to your resources."

"Done." He interrupted her speech to let her know her first condition was acceptable. "Next!" he said, nudging her to belch out the second condition.

"You let me use a phone so as to say goodbye." He stretched his arm out and one of the men handed him a satellite phone. He then opened the glass cage of her enclosure symbolising her freedom of movement and handed her the phone.

Agent Archer Brown and his men had fairly ten minutes left before they would breach the compound. The formation had been laid out. As soon as the armoured vehicle would ram the gate, the men on each side of the wall would rush in. Those on the left side 'Alpha Team' would clear the left wing of the premises and those on the right 'Bravo Team' would clear the right wing while a third team 'Charlie' would be in the back of the vehicle, ready to exit as soon as the car came to a halt with a breaching device to break down the door, giving them access to the main house. Dionysus would then come in last after the area was secure.

"On the count of five," the unit commander spoke on his earpiece. "Five! Four! Three! Two! BREACH! BREACH! BREACH!" The armoured vehicle rammed through the gate and it flung open, blowing through its hinges, and just as they feared, Fulgar's men would not come easy. Projectiles pinged off the bulletproof car as Team Alpha and Bravo came rushing in with guns blazing. The men leading the charge fell as bullets started flying from all directions. "Take cover!" The unit commander ordered the men to find shelter from the firefight. Team Charlie was still in the vehicle and under enemy's suppressing fire so they couldn't exit the car to carry out their duties. One of Fulgar's men armed with a rocket-propelled grenade 'RPG' fired at the fuel tank of the armoured car. *SSSSSSS... BOOM!* The vehicle exploded in a huge ball of flames and all its occupants, Agent Archer Brown being one of them, were burned alive. Their screams could be heard from miles away. It was absolute chaos.

Dionysus was no stranger to such a hostile environment. He was planning on going around the compound, as the breach would have served as distraction and the entrance a point of focus. "I need two men to reconvene on me. I'm flanking the compound," he spoke on the earpiece he was given.

"Copy that," the unit commander responded. "I need the person closest to the exit from each team to reconvene at Dionysus's location while we lay down suppressing fire. Five! Four! Three! Two! GO! GO! GO!" *BRAPAP! BRAPAP! BRAPAP!* They returned fire in three round burst shots at the assailants who seemed to have a full vantage point and the high-ground advantage as some were on the second floor of the main structure. The compound would have passed for a battleground.

While they made their way to where he was taking cover, his phone rang. He was about to hang up due to the timing of it all, but then he remembered that he had only given that number to one person to reach out to him during emergencies. He had no doubt in his mind who was on the other side of the call even before he answered it, of which he quickly did. "Hello."

"Forgive me, Father, for I have sinned," she said poetically, reminding him of the first time they met each other.

"Are you okay? Are you hurt?"

"No, I'm fine. Glad you are in one piece as well. I thought they killed you."

"No, I'm fine," he responded to keep her at ease and objective. "I need you to tell me where they are keeping you. What can you see around you?" he asked, eagerly awaiting her response so as to get a rough idea of where in the compound she was being held.

"That's not important right now," she replied, much to his dismay. The men who had made it to Dionysus's location furiously asked him to hang up the phone and get his head in the fight, unaware who was on the other side of the call. He gave them a shooing gesture, indicating that they should go ahead without him.

"I knew we shouldn't have brought a civilian into this," one of the men said as they both proceeded at the task to flank the enemy.

"I'm calling to say goodbye. There have been some horrific developments on my end and I cannot in good faith bring you into this world. You have been my knight in shining armour, my protector, and my happiness after countless years of life without colour, but now I must go. Whenever you think of me, remember I wasn't taken from you. I left. Please don't look for me and try and move on with your life. I will never forget you, and for me, never is a long time. Goodbye!"

"Genevieve, wait!" Dionysus shouted but she had already hung up the phone.

He got on his motorcycle, as it was a quicker option and he would soon catch up with the men who left him behind in order to flank the compound. "We must leave now!" Fulgar took the phone from Genevieve as Cassim arrived, winded. "We have to go now!" He handed him what appeared to be a gladius and she thought nothing of it and assumed it to be a memento of sorts. They made their way to the underground tunnel she saw the men run into. It turned out it was an emergency exit. She could smell the fresh air and had no doubt in her mind that if they kept moving in the direction they were moving in, they would be outdoors, soon free and clear to escape.

"God fall?" he asked Cassim as they walked in an alarmingly calm manner considering that they were under siege.

"Done, sir," he responded. 'God fall' was the code for a contingency plan they had laid out for when the compound would be breached. It involved a mass evacuation of his men and whatever resources they could transport and a few men who would sacrifice themselves by keeping the authorities occupied in a firefight and dying in battle either by their hand or the authorities as the rest escaped through the underground tunnel. Once they were in the wind, the whole place was rigged with enough explosives to leave a crater on the ground once set off! Cassim, Genevieve, and Fulgar were the last people left to exit the compound. The rest of his group of terrible men used the thirty-minute window to make a hasty escape, taking the hounds and weapons with them and driving off with a fleet of black vans with diplomatic plates that guaranteed that they would not be pulled over in roadblocks as soon as 'God fall' was initiated.

They were soon at the exit where a black SUV with diplomatic plates awaited them. "FREEZE! DON'T MOVE!" they heard as they were about to board the vehicle. The two men who had taken it upon themselves to go around the compound had caught up to Fulgar's exit strategy and now had him and Cassim dead to rights with their rifles pointed at them. Cassim was about to make a move when Fulgar touched his shoulder, indicating that he would take care of the situation. "Get in the car," he told Genevieve as Cassim joined her, leaving Fulgar at gunpoint with the men. He looked at Genevieve who was staring at the events unfold from the car and smiled.

"Don't do it," she whispered beneath her breath. He could make out what she was saying but ignored her. "His eyes! His eyes! NO! GOD, NO!" she said in terror as Fulgar showed her his true form, the white in his eyes had turned pitch-black!

"YOU DARE POINT YOUR GUNS AT ME!" he yelled, his voice was deep and distorted, much like the dark entity's! His gladius that he held in his hand and she thought to be a memento caught ablaze with what she presumed to be the flames of hell! They opened fire at him in pure terror, the bullets making a thud upon impact and him slowly advancing towards them, unfazed. Without injury and a menacing smile on his face, he vanished into a thick cloud of dark smoke and reappeared inches away from where the men were standing, hacking and slicing away vanishing and reappearing almost as if toying with them. Their screams filled the air until all there was, was silence, human parts on the ground, and a gladius-wielding, blood-drenched Fulgar standing over what was left of their dismembered corpses.

"As mine is lust, his is war," Genevieve repeated the dark entity's quote in terror as she processed the display of Fulgar's frightening ability. "His is war," she whispered under her breath reiterating the thoughts on her new associate as they drove off and Cassim handed him what appeared to be a remote detonator. After a few minutes on the road, he looked back at her with an evil grin and flipped the switch on the device in his hand!

Dionysus revved the motorcycle at its maximum engine capabilities as he attempted to catch up with the men who went before him. He arrived like a God from a machine with his weapon drawn only to find what was left of them. She was gone and with her his heart. He attempted to pursue them in the direction of their tire tracks but was thrown into a thicket thirty feet away by a shockwave that soon followed the loudest bang he had ever heard in all his war-filled years!

****